TENDERFOOT

DUDE

OTHER BOOKS BY THE AUTHOR

Non-fiction:

Voices from Prison, Tate Publishing, Inc., 2014

Memoir:

Between the Devil and the Deep...Memoir of a Maverick Priest, Butterfly Creations, Xlibris, 2010

Sailing Books:

Cruising Definition, Butterfly Creations, 2011
Cruising Prayer Book, Butterfly Creations, 1991
Bitter End Songbook, Butterfly Creations, 1986

The author has also written several technical books regarding prisons.

TENDERFOOT DUDE

By Ames K. Swartsfager

NOTE

This book is a work of fiction and names, places, persons, locations, and anything else you can think of came purely from my imagination. The only exception to the above is that I am a grandfather and I have two grandchildren whose names are Austin and Rachael, and I do tell stories at the drop of the proverbial hat.

Published by BUTTERFLY CREATIONS

Printed by Create Space, An Amazon Company.

Type Font is Georgia, 11.5 point

Cover by Joeseph Keeny

ISBN-13: 978-0-9827580-3-8

ACKNOWLEDGMENTS

I first have to thank Rachael and Austin Hernandez, my great but sometimes irascible grandchildren, for listening to my stories without, most of the time, nodding off. I would also thank my writers group (Carol, Pam, Mike, Lou, and Debra) for their advice—even though they made me change the name of an important character when I was almost finished writing it.

Special thanks to Joseph Keeny for creating the cover for this book.

I am most thankful that I have a great wife, who encourages me, edits my writing and has stuck with me for 56 years, of which 50 of them have been great.

DEDICATION

This book is for the cowboys and cowgirls who in real life or in their imaginations roam the wild ranges in search of adventure.

Table of Contents

GRANDPA: Prelude

"Aw, please, grandpa, please," pleaded Rachael, her round face mournful and her head cocked. As usual, she was using her blue eyes and long blond hair in an attempt to manipulate her grandfather into telling a story about his youth. "Please, just one story?"

They were sitting around a campfire on their back patio, making s'mores.

"I'll make you a huge s'more if you will." Rachael, a vivacious nine-year old, was trying to bribe her grandpa who was more than a little overweight and liked to eat. She also had the habit of rubbing his grey beard just to annoy him.

Grandpa, whose real name was Jack Elliott, looked over to Austin, a hefty fourteen-year-old, who had a strange look on his face. He knew what Austin was thinking. He was attempting to make a choice: a story from grandpa or back to his ever present X-game.

"Well, Austin," grandpa said. "Do you want to hear a story?"

"I'm not sure. Will it be a good story, grandpa?"

"It is true," thought grandpa. "Sometimes my stories are boring."

"I think it will be interesting. It has cowboys, ghosts, rustlers, and it is a semi-true story that really might have happened. But you don't have to stay. You may leave at any time"

Austin hesitated and shifted in his chair. "I guess I'll stay."

"Can we make s'mores while you tell it?" Rachael asked with a flip of her blond hair.

"Sure." He settled back into his cushioned patio chair. "Now this story takes place a long time ago, when I was just a little snapper–just twelve years old—1951. We lived in small town called Bryan, Texas."

"Was that before there were cars?" gibed Austin, as he stuck another marshmallow on the end of his willow stick.

"No, we had cars, but we didn't have television in the town yet, and air conditioning was unknown. We ran around barefoot from the day school was over until the day school began–except for Sundays. We were forced to wear shoes to church.

"Our story begins in January, I think. Maybe it was February."

CHAPTER ONE: Unexpected Encounter

Jack Elliott ran to get the door. His sixteen year old sister was expecting her date and he wanted to see the guy who was brave enough to take her out. Opening the door, he came face to face with two buckles on a tooled cowboy belt. His eyes moved upwards past a checkered Western style shirt to a tall, tough, youngish man, with a face which already seemed lined with wisdom.

"Good evening," said the young man, taking off a grey Stetson, the ultimate cowboy hat. He placed it over his heart and gave a little bow. "I'm Frank Rollin. Is Dianne in?"

"Who's Dianne?" interrupted Rachael.

"Don't you remember your great aunt Dianne?"

"Oh yeah. I remember her now."

"Let's get back to the story. Let's see..."

"Oh my!" Jack thought. *"My sister's got her a cowboy."*

He looked down and saw, jutting out from faded stovepipe blue jeans, a pair of polished but well-worn cowboy boots.

"Excuse me," the cowboy requested again, politely. "Is Dianne home?"

"Yes," Jack stammered, filled with awe at being in the presence of a real cowboy. Ever since he saw his first cowboy movie, Jack had wanted to be a cowboy. He was overjoyed when the Elliott family moved to Texas in 1950. They had arrived just in time to start school, but he had yet to meet a real cowboy. The way the movies depicted the West, everyone in Texas was a cowboy. He knew some men who wore cowboy boots were not the real thing. They wore them just for show. This was the first real cowboy he had seen in person.

"Come in. Have a seat. I'm Jack, Dianne's brother," he said, then ran down the hallway to his sister's room.

"Dianne, your boyfriend is here!" Jack yelled through the closed door. He used the word boyfriend because he knew it would rile her.

"Shut up, Jack," Dianne responded in anger. "Tell him I'll be out soon. And don't call him my 'boyfriend!'"

Jack went back to the living room and sat across from his

16

new idol. He couldn't help staring at Frank. He was close shaven with lines around his eyes from squinting at the sun while herding cattle on the back of his palomino horse, Jack knew for sure. Yet he also knew that he must be only eighteen or nineteen years old or his sister would not have been allowed to date him. Frank had an easy smile and Jack liked him at first sight, even though he was dating his dumb sister.

"May I get you something to drink, Mr. Rollin?" Jack asked timidly.

"Naw, Jack," he replied. "Please call me Frank. What's your favorite game?"

"I like shooting marbles best of all." Jack was a fair marble shooter and had a large bag of winnings to prove it.

"That's great, Jack. Have you ever played poker?"

If Jack had not believed he was a true cowboy before, this proved it. In the movies, the cowboys always played poker in their spare time.

"No. I don't know how to play poker, but I'd like to learn."

"Great. I'll show you. Do you have a deck of cards?"

Jack ran and got the cards out of the dining room drawer, praying his sister would take her time. Frank shuffled the cards expertly, ruffling them forward and backward.

"Can you show me how to do that, Frank?"

"Sure, but let's learn the game first." He explained the order of succession, from a pair to a royal flush. "Ready to play?" he asked as he started dealing the cards face down.

17

"Five card draw is the easiest one to start with."

They started playing and, to Jack's surprise, he was winning. Pennies were used to bet, and Frank even supplied Jack five to start with.

In the midst of a game, Dianne appeared in all her glory, but Frank was intent on a decision to raise or just meet Jack's bet. Jack saw, out of the corner of his eye, Dianne begin to fume. Whenever she became angry she turned red around her neck and face, which spoiled her rather pretty looks. Dianne had a nice smile when she used it, long brunette hair and brown eyes. She was even wearing her best spring dress. It was yellow with little green butterflies. Even Jack had to admit, though he'd never tell her, she looked good in it.

A few minutes later, when the play was finished, Frank stood.

"Dianne, I hope you will excuse me for being so engrossed in the poker game. I was just teaching your brother." Frank's speech flowed with a soft Texan drawl that was smooth. It seemed to placate Dianne.

"That's all right," she said with a blush and her best smile. "I'm sorry I was late getting ready."

"Are you ready to go?" Frank asked.

Dianne nodded, and Jack said to Frank, "Wait. Let me return the money you lent me to play with."

"Never mind Jack," Frank said. "You won it square. Save it for next time."

After they left, Jack went and looked into the full length

mirror in the hall. What he saw was a kid wearing flannel pants and a short sleeved shirt. He attempted to picture himself dressed in a Stetson hat and he sighed. His big ears sticking out from his head would spoil its looks. Jack's hazel eyes were his best feature, he thought. He felt his cheeks for hair, but there was nothing he could shave yet. And he was short. Jack knew he would never be as tall as Frank. But wasn't Billy the Kid short? Maybe with cowboy boots on, he might look taller. Sighing again, he knew he would never be a cowboy.

To Dianne's consternation, they played poker every time Frank came over.

He discovered that the faster he disappeared right after Dianne came out the more money he won. So Jack made a habit of going to the corner drug store for a cherry phosphate. He figured if Frank wanted to let him win, it was not his problem.

"What's a cherry phosphate?" Austin asked.

"That was like a cherry soda, but was best known for curing an uneasy stomach. I liked it better than a cherry coke. Now, back to the story."

The next few months Jack and Frank became good friends. Frank was finishing his freshman year at Texas A & M and told Jack stories of the hazing he had to undergo as a freshman. "The seniors beat the juniors, the juniors beat the

19

sophomores, and the sophomores beat the freshmen. Well," he sighed, "after this year I'll only have two years to go before I'm out of it all."

During one of many poker games, Frank told of his experiences on the ranch. Jack listened wide eyed to every word. Cutting out cattle, branding the new calves, the annual roundup were all very interesting, but the story that stuck most in his mind was the ghost.

"We've had some trouble over the past two years because our herd seems to be getting smaller rather than larger. I think we have rustlers that are somehow stealing our cattle. But according to some of our ranch hands, a ghost has been taking them." Frank laughed as Jack dealt another poker hand.

"A ghost?" Jack stopped dealing and looked Frank in the eyes, attempting to find out if he was being teased. "You really mean it?"

"I'm not kidding," Frank continued as he looked through the cards in his new hand. "This ghost is supposed to be Don Cuerno de Vaca, a Spanish grandee who owned most of southwest Texas. When the Texas Republic overthrew Mexico, Cuerno de Vaca was killed in the fighting and his land was divided and sold." Frank threw two cards face down. "I'll have two," he continued as Jack considered his own hand.

"My great, great, great grandfather bought a lot of this land and we still own some of it."

Jack threw down three cards, dealt Frank two and

20

himself three. "And?" he asked as he looked at his new cards.

Frank was quiet for a few minutes as he considered his hand. He frowned and then continued. "And over the years there have been many sightings of Cuerno de Vaca riding across the range on a ghostly white horse. Some have even said they hear him moaning near the corral on nights when the moon is full."

Jack raised his bet and asked, "Did you ever hear the ghost?"

"Nope, I never did," Frank said, raised his bet again and called. Jack revealed his hand and grinned. Three aces were staring up from the table.

"Got ya!" said Frank as he placed three deuces and two sevens next to Jack's cards. "I knew you would fall for that frown I gave you. Never trust the face of your opponent. Bluffing is part of the game." Frank picked up seven cents, his winnings. "Anyway, I think it's all rubbish."

"Bluffing?" asked Jack, confused.

"No, partner," Frank continued, beginning to shuffle the cards. "I don't believe the ghost story."

That night Jack dreamed that a ghost wearing armor and riding a white horse was chasing him. He got so near Jack could hear the armor clatter and clang as Don Cuerno de Vaca galloped after him. Jack knew he was doomed. He turned and looked over his shoulder as he tried to run even faster. The ghost was nearing him, his long white goatee blowing back over his armor, his mouth in rictus, a silent grin and coals of fire burning in his vacant eyes.

Jack woke up in a sweat. He punched his pillow and pulled the covers over his head.

CHAPTER TWO: Kid's Belt!

One Sunday in May, Frank dropped by to see Dianne, but first he asked to talk to Jack alone. They went out onto the front porch.

"I've got a problem," he said. "You know that all freshmen have to go to ROTC training in the summer. So I'll have to go. But this will leave my father one cowpoke short. Would you consider coming to the ranch and maybe riding the fence or something?"

"Would I consider? . . . Consider?" Jack thought. He did not know what riding fence was, but here was his chance to be a real cowboy.

"Yes . . . sure . . . of course," Jack said, filled with expectation. "But...what is riding fence?"

"That's when someone rides around the fence line looking for breaks in the fence so cattle won't escape."

"That sounds like an important job."

"It is, but I'll have to talk to your father first," Frank said.

That evening when Frank brought Dianne back from the Saturday matinee, he and Jack's father went into the study and talked for a long time. Jack attempted to listen but heard only a mumble. Praying and hoping as he never had before he asked, "Please God, let Dad agree to let me become a cowboy."

When his father came out of the study, Jack could tell nothing from his face. However, Frank was failing at trying not to smile.

"Well?" Jack could not take the suspense.

"Well what?" his father questioned, and this time Jack could see him struggling with a smile that wanted to escape.

"Can I go to Frank's ranch and learn to be a cowboy?" Jack did not look directly at his father for fear of seeing a negative reaction.

"That depends on Mr. Rollin, Frank's father. If he agrees, and you really want to . . . .."

"Oh, I do!" Jack broke in.

"Then you have my permission to go. But you know it won't be easy."

"That's right," Frank said. "It's darn hard work."

"I can do it – I know I can!"

The next two weeks seemed more like a year. At last, the letter arrived inviting Jack to join the cowboys at the Rollin R Ranch (®➜). In the letter was a list of things he would have to bring:

1. Three pairs of blue jeans, one good pair of pants for church or parties.

2. Five long-sleeved shirts.

3. One good shirt.

4. Heavy socks - at least ten pairs.

5. Warm jacket.

6. Riding cowboy boots - pointed toes and high heels so the foot can easily grip the stirrup.

7. Dress shoes - cowboy boots with low heels and wider toes will do.

8. Underwear and one set of "long johns" for night work.

9. Hunting knife.

10. Hat with broad brim to keep the sun off.

Just reading this list set Jack's imagination off. He pictured himself in his Stetson, jeans and checkered shirt, sitting on a horse singing to the herd at night. Shivers went up his spine.

Jack did not get a Stetson after all. It was too expensive, but the hat he got was nice. It was flat topped, black with a broad brim. If Jack were to be in a movie, this hat would identify him as a bad guy. He did not get the second pair of boots either – for the same reason. However, his shirts were western style and, after buying the jeans, he ran home and filled the tub with hot water, put a pair on and sat in the tub for an hour.

"You did what?" Rachael asked just before a s'more went into her mouth.

"In those days the jeans were baggy and they shrank a lot, so we would put them on and sit in hot water. This would shrink them almost skin tight. They had another problem though. A lot of the blue dye would leak out."

Jack's mother was furious because the tub turned blue by the time Jack had soaked all three pairs. He spent the next two hours scrubbing the tub with scouring powder. Those jeans, though, fit him like a glove and when he put them on with his boots, shirt and hat, Jack saw that he looked a little like an old experienced cow poke. Only one thing was missing–the belt.

"I have to get a new belt," Jack told his mother at dinner that night. She did not answer, but looked at Mr. Elliott.

"I have to have a new belt, Dad. I need one like the cowboys wear: with several buckles and special leather tooling all around."

"I'm sorry, Jack," his Father said. "We just can't afford to buy anything else at this time. You'll just have to make do with the old belt."

Jack knew it would not help to plead with his Father. Nevertheless, he was embarrassed to have to wear a kid's belt.

"It's getting late, kids. Time for bed. Besides, the mosquitoes are eating me alive."

Oh, grandpa!" Rachael pleaded. "Just five minutes more."

"Yes, please," added Austin. "I want to know what's going to happen."

"Tomorrow night we will continue the story. It gets very funny later on. Now to bed and don't forget to pick up the wrappers from the Hershey bars and marshmallows on your way in."

CHAPTER THREE - Outlaws and Indians

"Jack, stop day dreaming and get back to studying." Mrs. McCartney, his math teacher, woke him up. Jack could only think of one thing lately–riding the range.

The last weeks of school dragged by, like the last few days before Christmas. Then when he was not ready, school ended. Two days later, Frank came to pick him up. He would have almost two weeks to teach Jack how to ride before he had to go to ROTC camp.

Dressed in his finest cowboy clothes, Jack swaggered to meet him. He had wanted to wear his new boots, but they were riding boots and he could hardly walk in them. He kept his old belt buckle covered with his hands, not wanting Frank to see it.

"Now don't you look just like a cowpoke? Take your hands away from your stomach and stand tall."

Reluctantly, Jack pulled his hands away and placed them along his sides. He felt his face turn red with embarrassment. The old belt had painted figures of the Lone Ranger. It was definitely a kid's belt. Jack wanted to run and hide.

"That belt won't do," Frank said. "All the hands will tease you to death. Why don't you try this on?" Frank reached into a bag he was holding and pulled out a brand new cowboy belt with real tooling and two silver buckles. Overcome with happiness, Jack almost cried, but instead he accepted the belt and put it on. Then he took the kid's belt and put it in the trash can. Jack knew deep in his soul that a new phase of life had just started.

They got into Frank's old black Ford pickup and headed down the road. Both were silent for awhile, but Jack's mind wasn't quiet. Pictures of cowboys and Indians, outlaws, and even barroom brawls flitted through his mind.

"There are some things you should know." Frank's voice intruded on Jack's day dreams. "The old hands always tease the newest cowboy in the outfit. It's just a natural thing. Don't let it get you down."

Frank went on to tell about the special horse every ranch had. It was always given to the newest cowpoke to test his ability to ride.

"Our 'special' horse is Mabel. If they give you Mabel to ride, ask for another horse. Mabel is funny. She trots along just fine for awhile, then for no reason she'll throw her rider, walk a few paces more and begin to graze as if nothing happened. Mabel will give her rider no warning. One cowhand quit after spending a day with her. He probably wasn't the kind of man we wanted anyway. So be prepared for teasing."

"OK," Jack said, "I won't let it bother me, but..."

"But what?"

"Well, are there any Indians . . . or outlaws there?" As soon as the words came out of his mouth he regretted them.

"Yes, Jack, there is at least one Indian. His name is Begay . . . James Begay, a Navajo Indian." Frank turned and looked at Jack, suppressing a smile. "He's a quiet man, but a first rate cowpoke. If you ever get to know him you'll like him." He paused a minute thinking. "As for outlaws, maybe."

"You mean," Jack blurted out, "there really are outlaws there?"

"Well now, Jack," he said, "there just might be. We've been losing cattle, but we don't know how they take them. Not a trace is left behind. As I said before, some say that the ghost of Don Cuerno de Vaca, whose family owned the place in the seventeenth century, is taking them." He laughed, "But it's just rustlers. That's why I don't want to go to ROTC training camp this summer. Thought I might be able to discover the culprits. But I can't get out of ROTC."

"Wait a minute. What's ROTC?" Austin asked.

"That means Reserve Officer's Training Course.

31

They still have it at Texas A & M and I took it when I was in high school. I don't think they have it there anymore."

"Wow! Rustlers!" Jack was excited now. "Maybe I can find them."

"No, Jack, don't even go that way. It's too dangerous." Frank removed his Stetson and wiped his forehead with a red checked handkerchief. "My father and the hands will eventually find out who it is taking them."

It was hot in the pickup, even with the windows down. The truck was traveling through the flat southwest Texas plains area. You could see for miles around. There were little groups of cattle standing under trees. There were sage, small cactus and scrub bushes everywhere.

"Where are the tall cactus that look like stick men?" Jack asked, remembering the cowboy movies.

"They don't grow here, only in Arizona. By the way, if someone asks you to sit on a plant that looks like a foot stool, don't. It's a cactus and you'll spend the rest of the summer pulling cactus spines out of your butt."

As the truck rolled along, Jack watched the scenery pass by. He didn't know what Frank was thinking, but he was trailing rustlers through canyons filled with cactus. Suddenly Frank turned the truck onto a dirt road.

"We're here." They turned off the road and passed under an archway with nothing but the symbol, ®➜. Frank was a little ahead of himself, it seemed, as it took another half hour to reach the ranch house. Really, it was a group of houses.

"Those building over there are the stables, bunk house, and a miscellaneous animal barn."

"What's a miscellaneous animal barn?"

"Oh, we have some pigs, chickens and cows to provide food and milk for the ranch," Frank slid out of the truck and slammed the door. Jack followed his example.

"Slamming the door," Frank explained, "is like a door bell here." They stretched and went to the back of the truck and unloaded the gear. By the time they turned around, Jack was met by a round face smiling woman, who seemed a little older than his mother. Her hair was graying, but he could see the remnants of blond hair shining in the sunlight. She had it tied up in a knot on her head. She wore blue jeans and a short sleeved checkered shirt. Jack liked her as soon as he saw her blue eyes, which smiled at him.

"This must be Jack," she said in greeting. "You're bigger than I thought you'd be. Welcome to the Rollin R Ranch," she said, sticking out her hand. "Glad to have you here."

"Hi," Jack said lamely as he tried to stand a little taller. He took her hand. "I'm very happy to be here and I thank you for the invitation." His father would have been proud of his courtesy.

"Jack," he had commanded, "You be polite now, and don't embarrass the family."

They walked toward the large doorway, which was obviously the main house. It was a long one story building, painted light tan. The roof, made of red tiles, was built out over the walls a few feet. In front and around it were cactus and flower beds. There was not much in the way of grass, but it was pleasant enough. There were several large oak trees giving shade to the front of the house.

From the house came a short, bent over, old Chinese man.

"This is Chan," said Mrs. Rollin, introducing the man who was dressed in a blue Chinese smock and wore a black round box-like hat on his head. "He'll take your bags."

"That's all right," Jack said, picking up his duffle bag and suitcase. He did not want an old man to do his job. Evidently Frank concurred as he also picked up his gear after giving his mother a hug and a kiss.

Jack could not believe how elegant and cool it was inside. The walls of the huge living room were paneled with a dark wood. Light came in through the high windows and cast shadows around the room. Along one wall was a fireplace so large Jack thought someone could stand up in it and still not hit his head. There were chairs with leather and rawhide coverings. Jack could imagine being here on a cold night, huddled up to a blazing fire. As it was, though, he shivered. It was hot outside, at least ninety-five degrees, but it was very cool inside.

Mrs. Rollin saw Jack shiver and said, "We don't have air conditioning, Jack. But the walls are thick and that keeps us cool in the summer and warm in the winter. If you are cold, you might want to get a sweater."

"No," Jack said, "I'm fine." He was hoping that this welcome would not go on long as he needed to pee and didn't want to ask where the bathroom was.

"Well, you both must be tired. Richard Senior should be back in by dinner. Why don't you both go to your rooms and rest until then? We'll put Jack in the room next to yours, Frank."

They went down a long hallway, turned a corner and continued down another hall. Jack was getting weary toting his bags.

"How much farther is it?" Jack asked. "This place is huge."

"It's not really so far," Frank said, giving a hitch to his luggage. "Generally we take a short cut across the patio. I'll show you later."

Frank stopped at a door. "This will be your room. It's right next to mine."

He opened the door to the room. It was a bright room, with a French door leading to the patio. Light airy drapes could be pulled across the door/window for privacy. The bed stood against a wall, and over it, attached to the wall, was one of the most colorful serapes Jack had even seen. Across from the bed was a wash stand and, next to that, a closet in a cabinet. Jack opened the door and looked in. It was empty except for a few hangers.

"In the days in which this house was built, about 1906 I

think, it was easier to use a cabinet for a closet than to build one in as they do today," Frank said, noting Jack's curiosity.

"Frank," Jack said tentatively, "Do we have to rest? All I have to do is go to the bathroom, and then I want to see the horses and everything."

"All right, partner." Frank smiled and opened a door at the end of Jack's bed. "We share this bathroom. Knock on my door when you're finished. Then we'll both explore."

CHAPTER FOUR: Enter the Redhead

They left the house through Jack's bedroom door to the patio, cooled by the shade of several huge pecan and oak trees. The roof overhung a paved walk along the side of the house. The two walked along another path that led to the center of the patio, where a large bubbling fountain in a pond stood at the crossing of two walkways.

"The fountain is fed by an artesian well. There aren't many of these in Texas," Frank said with pride. "That's why they built the house here, for the fresh water. The water is still piped in from the well."

"This place is beautiful. It's so cool and nice."

"When it gets over a hundred degrees this summer, it still seems cool here. We frequently eat out here in the evening."

Jack looked at the lush green plants and trees, "I've never seen a house built around a patio like this," Jack observed.

"The house was built in a square like this to protect

against Indian raids," Frank said as he led Jack out of a gate and toward the stables. "We only put the outside windows in twenty years ago."

They entered the stables from a side door. Jack was greeted with the smell of horse, horse droppings, and straw. It was dark and cool here also. The stable seemed to be a block long with stalls along both sides. He could hear the horses moving around in their stalls. Jack wondered which horse would be his.

"This is Mabel, the horse I told you about. Never ride her," Frank warned with a chuckle.

Jack laughed nervously, remembering what Frank had said in the truck and wishing he would hurry and show him the horse he would ride. Instead, Frank went from stall to stall. When there was a horse in a stall, he introduced it to Jack.

"Barnaby," Frank said, "This is Jack. Jack, meet Barnaby."

"Hi, Barnaby," Jack said, feeling foolish. The horse came over and nuzzled Frank's hand.

"Horses are like humans," Frank explained, moving past an empty stall. "They like to know who's going to ride them."

Frank came to a stall with a horse that had big black and white spots on it. Her ears were perked up and she had the largest brown eyes Jack had ever seen. They stopped at the stall window and the horse ambled over and shoved Frank's shoulder with her nose.

"This is Star, Jack. She's a Pinto," he said, rubbing the horse's ears. "She was named because of this." Frank pointed to a black spot on her chest that had what looked like a white star in the middle. "We're old friends. Star will be one of your horses."

"One of my horses?"

"Every cowhand has a string of horses, and you will have two. I'll explain later. But Star will be the one you learn to ride on." The horse moved her head and nudged Jack's arm. Star's head was huge and he was frightened, but when Star nudged him a second time, Jack reached out and rubbed the top of her nose. The horse stomped her fore hoof with pleasure. When Jack stopped rubbing, Star moved her head farther out from the stall and nodded. It was as if she was saying "Yes, more."

Jack rubbed between her ears as Frank had done. He was beginning to relax and knew that Star and he would be good friends.

"She likes you," Frank said. He handed Jack a piece of carrot. "Give her this, but keep your hand flat when you hand it to her. Otherwise you might lose a few fingers."

Jack placed the piece of carrot on his hand and held it out to Star. The horse's soft lips lifted it from Jack's hand and, with a toss of her head, it was gone. Star nodded her head again, wanting more.

"We've got to move on if we are going to see the barn. Don't want to be late for dinner. Father wouldn't like that."

Walking across a gravel and dirt yard toward the large barn, Jack could not stop looking around. Everything was new and different.

"How big is this ranch?" Jack asked.

"We have about 250,000 acres. Used to be bigger, but Father told me we sold off 100,000 acres back in the thirties when times were tough." Frank opened the small door that was set into the larger door of the weathered red barn. The barn also had a smell like the stables, yet it was different. More pungent.

"What's that up there?" Jack asked. "A balcony?"

"That's a hay loft. It's just a place where we store hay and straw for the livestock. When I was young I used to sneak up there for a nap," Frank laughed. "Hardly anyone would expect to find me there.

"We keep a few milk cows for use on the ranch. We also have pigs, chickens and turkeys, especially in the fall for Thanksgiving and Christmas dinners. The beef we get from our cattle. We are almost self sufficient," Frank said with pride.

They walked back to the house in silence, Jack still trying to absorb all he had seen. But most of all, his mind was on Star, his horse. He would ride a horse. He would be a cowboy.

After washing up and changing into clean clothes, they headed for the dining room.

"Do you always get so dressed up for dinner?" Jack asked.

"It's a family tradition," Frank said. "We always put clean clothes on for dinner. Otherwise we would smell like sweat and horses. Mom says she doesn't allow horses, or horse smelling people, at her table."

The family gathered around a long, rough hewn table made smooth by thousands of dinners. It was fifteen feet long. When they entered the dining room, Mrs. Rollin was placing huge bowls of food on the table.

"We're having Frank Junior's favorite dinner. Steak, mashed potatoes and gravy, carrots with onions, and a tossed salad." she said. "Of course, I baked some fresh rolls and three apple pies."

"Gee, that's a lot of food," Jack said, eyeing the large bowls and platters.

"Not for my men it isn't." Mrs. Rollin adjusted some silverware. "And don't forget, you're one of my men now." A beautiful smile broke out on her face.

Just when Jack was going to reply, a man entered the room. His face was crinkled like sun baked earth. Tall, at least six-foot-two inches, and thin. His forearms protruding from his checkered shirt showed he was wiry and strong. Although his hair was grey, he seemed youthful. Around his full mustache one could see a smile flickering.

He went over to Frank and gave him a big bear hug. "You look like a man, by heavens. I knew that Texas A & M would make a man of you." He slapped Frank on the back, and then turned to Jack. He reached out a huge calloused hand and grabbed Jack's in a strong, but not painful, grip. He did not look like a man who had a large ranch. He was wearing clean faded jeans and a red checkered long sleeved shirt with the cuffs rolled back.

"I'm Frank's father. You must be Jack. Welcome to the Rollin R."

"Thank you sir," Jack said. "I really appreciate being invited. It's a huge place."

"It's big enough," Mr. Rollin said, grinning. Then he went and sat at the head of the table. Frank showed Jack where to sit. Just as he started to sit down, another man entered. He was not as tall as Frank Senior, but he looked very tough.

"Buddy," said Mr. Rollin, "this is our new hand, Jack. He'll be with us this summer. I don't know why, but Jack wants to be a cowpoke."

Buddy looked at Jack strangely, his grey eyes staring through him. "You sure you want to be a cowboy?" he asked.

"Yes sir," Jack said trying to be confident and taking the outstretched hand. Buddy's sunburned face changed into a smile. As he went to sit down, Jack noticed a circle was rubbed into the back pocket of his jeans.

"What's that?" Jack whispered to Frank. "The circle on his jean pocket."

"Oh that's where he keeps his can of snuff," Frank whispered back. "Lots of the men use snuff."

"Buddy is the foreman here," Frank Senor interjected. "He knows everything about being a cow hand. You can learn a lot from him."

Jack sat down, the smell of food making his mouth water. The mashed potatoes were right in front of him. He wanted to dig into the bowl without waiting.

"Is she late again?" Mr. Rollin asked his wife in an annoyed tone.

"She'll be..." Mrs. Rollin started to say when a red headed girl fairly flew into the room and into her seat. She was very pretty and her green eyes sparkled as she spoke.

"Wait a minute, grandpa," Rachael said. "Why can't the girl be blond and have blue eyes?"

"Is this your story or is it mine? You want to take over?"

"Oh no, grandpa. Please continue.

"The girl was a redhead with flashing green eyes, okay?"

There was a moment of silence. Then he continued.

"I'm sorry, grandpa, I was playing with the new chicks. They're so cute. Hi, Uncle Frank." Then she turned to Jack, "Who is this?"

"Jack," said Frank, "This is my niece, Ann."

"Hi," was all he had a chance to say before they were called to silence as Mr. Rollin prayed over the food.

During the blessing, Jack's thoughts were not on God but

on the long red hair and the deep green eyes of the girl sitting across from him. She looked very pretty in her jeans and green checkered shirt. Jack wondered how old she was. Not that he was that interested in girls, but this one intrigued him.

There was not much talk as the group ate their steaks. It was not until after Jack had eaten two big pieces of the apple pie that the real conversation began. It revolved around ranch business mostly and Jack had no idea what they meant by "herd reduction" and "projected calf rate." They talked about losses mostly.

"How many unbranded heifers have we lost?" Mr. Rollin inquired of his foreman.

Buddy thought for awhile, running his hand over his almost bald head. "Hard to tell, Mr. Rollin. We projected a twenty percent increase, but it doesn't seem that much to me. More like twelve or fifteen percent this year, but we won't really know until after the roundup." He shook his head slowly. "I tell you, the only thing that accounts for that is rustlers."

"Now Buddy, let's not get into that," said Mr. Rollin. He took a drink of coffee. "We need proof."

"Have we looked for foot prints, broken fences, and truck tracks?" Frank entered the conversation with a seriousness Jack had not seen before. "I wish I could be home this summer. I'd find out what's happening for sure."

"Frank," said Buddy, "we've done all that and more, but we have no leads at all."

"You don't believe in the ghost of Don Cuerno de Vaca, do you?" Frank sneered. Jack got the feeling that Frank did not like the foreman.

"Of course not," his father replied. "We'll keep looking and you will go to ROTC training camp. Besides, you have brought us help." He looked at Jack with a smile. "Maybe Jack can find out what's happening."

"Oh yes," scoffed Ann. "The tenderfoot dude really looks like he can find rustlers. What would you do when you found them, Jack?"

Jack could not believe Ann's rudeness and sarcasm. And what was a tenderfoot dude? His hands were shaking in anger. Jack felt like he had been attacked by this little snip of a redhead.

"All I want to do is learn how to work on a ranch," Jack blurted out, more loudly than he had intended, as he struggled to control his anger. "I have no idea how to find a rustler and, as Ann said, I wouldn't know what to do with one if I caught him." Everyone laughed while Ann turned red and began scraping crumbs off her dessert plate.

After dinner he and Frank went to the patio and sat.

"What is a 'tenderfoot dude,' Frank?" Jack was still hurting from Ann's barb.

"Well, a tenderfoot is a newcomer to ranching who is unfamiliar with our ways," Frank explained. "And a dude is someone who just wants to pretend he is a cowboy for a few weeks, hence 'Dude Ranches.' But don't mind Ann. She's really all right."

"I may be a tenderfoot," Jack said, "But I am not a dude. I don't want to pretend. I am going to be a cowboy."

"Well, don't pay any attention to her. She's a redhead and you never know what they're going to do. Outside of Ann, how do you like it here?"

"It's great! The food is so good that I'm afraid I'll turn into one of those pigs we saw this afternoon. By the way, what's snuff? You know, what the foreman uses."

"That is a way of using tobacco. It's in powder form and you put a pinch of it in your cheek." Frank demonstrated, taking a finger and pulling out his cheek. "It's really terrible stuff."

Ann arrived and joined them.

"Do you live here, Ann?" Jack asked, wanting to be friends.

"Naw, I've only been here a few weeks, but I spend every summer here with my grandparents. My home is in Abilene, Texas," she said. "Can you ride a horse, Jack?"

"Not yet, but I'll start learning tomorrow. Frank has promised to teach me."

"Great," Ann said with a smile that made anxiety rise up in Jack. "I'll come to the corral and watch."

CHAPTER FIVE: Boots and Saddles in the Old Corral

Just as Jack was sneaking up on the outlaws, one of them caught his shoulder. He wrestled with the stranger, trying to get the better of him. It was the ghost of Don Cuerno de Vaca. The masked apparition would not let go. In panic, Jack opened his eyes. Frank was shaking him.

"Hey Jack," he said with a grin, "It's time to get up."

The room was dark. He looked out the window and saw it was dark outside. Frank had already shaved and dressed.

"What time is it?" Jack moaned, rubbing the sleep from his eyes.

"Almost five. Hurry up; we have to be at breakfast in half an hour. And don't forget your boots."

Jack hurried dressing as fast as he could. He threw cold water on his face to wake up. It took him five minutes to get his new boots on and he found he could hardly walk. He wibboled and he wobbled, while Frank doubled over in laughter.

"Stop it, Frank," Jack pleaded. "I'm not used to wearing high heels. And my toes hurt."

When Frank could catch his breath he said, "It'll take some getting used to. Boots like these are not meant for walking, but they sure are helpful when riding. Now try to walk straight."

Jack walked around the room a few times, wishing he had practiced at home. He knew that if he walked funny, Ann would laugh. Very carefully and slowly, he entered the dining room and sat down as fast as he could. But it was too late.

Ann's eyes shined in laughter that had not reached her lips as yet. "Do your boots hurt, tenderfoot?" Then she laughed aloud. Jack's face turned red.

"Now Ann, leave the poor boy alone," Mrs. Rollin said. "He's new at this."

"You going to treat him like a baby?" Ann asked as she scooted her chair in.

"If the boy wants to learn cowpokin'," interrupted Mr. Rollin as he took his seat, "then let him learn it right. Nobody gets treated as a baby." He looked around the table. "Where's Buddy?"

"He told me he had to get an early start to check out things at the back bunkhouse," Mrs. Rollin said. "Probably not return until tomorrow evening."

"OK. Let's pray." Mr. Rollin began to say a blessing over

the food.

Jack paid no attention to the prayer. He was angry and vowed to get back at Ann. Chan soon had the table filled with platters of scrambled eggs, hash browns, sausage, bacon, and toast. Coffee, milk, and orange juice were placed on the table in carafes. And suddenly Jack was very hungry.

"After breakfast I'm going to give Jack his first riding lesson. He'll use Star to learn on."

"Isn't Star a little wild for him?" Mrs. Rollin had a worried expression on her face.

"She'll be good for Jack to learn on." Frank took a huge helping of eggs. "She's not too frisky, but she isn't passive either. After all, he'll have Kicker to ride later."

"I agree with Frank," Mr. Rollin said, buttering a hot buttermilk biscuit. "He will need to learn to ride, and fast. Jed, the new hand, is getting bored and we need him for herding. We need Jack to start riding fence next week."

As Jack filled his stomach, he mulled over the names of the horses. *Star sounded all right. But what about Kicker? How did he get that name?* Soon breakfast was over and they were headed for the stables. His knees felt weak and his hands shook.

When they arrived, Frank took him into what he called the "tack room."

"Here is where we keep all the saddles and bridles." As Jack looked around he saw saddles, ropes, blankets, and even trousers hanging from pegs. They were strange pants, as they had no back to them.

"These are chaps," Frank said, pulling down a short pair of the backless pants. "These should just fit you. They were mine at your age." He showed Jack how to belt them around the waist and clip them around the legs. "They will protect your jeans and your skin." He gave a little laugh.

Jack remembered seeing movie cowboys wearing these. He strutted around as much as he could with the boots on. Then Frank grabbed something he called a bridle and went to Star's stall. He made a clicking sound with his tongue. Star came and put her head though the window. Frank talked to her for a minute and then placed the bridle bit into her mouth, pulling the rest over her nose and ears.

"Hold the reins a minute, while I get your saddle."

Jack gulped down his nervousness and talked to Star, rubbing her nose. Frank came back with a blanket and saddle. "Let's bring her out." He set the saddle on the floor and opened the stall door.

Jack gave a little tug on the bridle to bring the horse out, but Star backed up instead.

"Don't let her do that, Jack. Give a hard jerk on the reins and walk backwards until she's out of the stall."

He did as Frank said and soon had Star out, but the horse kept moving around, tossing her head and snorting.

"Hold her steady," Frank instructed as he picked up the saddle and blanket. He threw the blanket over the horse, then the saddle. When the saddle landed heavily on Star, she moved to the side and almost got away.

"Steady," Frank said softly. Jack was not sure if Frank was talking to the horse or him. "Steady." Flipping the stirrup up onto the saddle, Frank reached under the horse and brought the cinch around Star's belly.

"Now this is the funny part. A horse will hold her breath when you cinch her so the strap won't be tight and later the saddle will fall off." He showed Jack how to pull it tight, wait for the horse to release his breath, and tighten the cinch again quickly.

Then Frank took the saddle and bridle off and told Jack to saddle the horse himself. After he had done that, Jack led Star out of the barn. Frank showed him how to mount on the left side. Then he adjusted the stirrups. Jack was torn between feeling excited about being on a horse he had saddled himself and being frightened about sitting on top of a live animal that had a mind of its own.

Frank grabbed the bridle and walked the horse into the corral. When Jack became used to sitting on Star, he looked around. Sitting on the rail right across from him was Ann. She was smiling.

Jack was on his own now, as Frank released the reins. The horse circled the corral.

"Steer with one hand," called Frank. Jack put the reins together, not really knowing how he was going to steer. "Lean into the turn." Jack leaned into a right turn and the next thing he knew Frank was picking him off the ground. Ann laughed so hard she almost fell off the fence. Jack wished she had.

"What happened?" he asked, a little dazed.

"You didn't get the cinch tight enough. Look at Star."

The horse was standing about ten feet from Jack. The saddle had slid almost under her and she looked humiliated. Frank helped Jack up and went over to the horse, straightened the saddle, and this time Jack cinched her three times.

Embarrassed, he was in a hurry to get on again, but attempted to mount the wrong side. Star shied away, Jack slipped and again he was on the ground. Ann howled with laughter, holding onto her sides. Trying to push Ann and her giggles out of his mind, Jack mounted Star correctly this time. Soon he began to understand what Frank was saying about steering with both reins in one hand.

"You may have to use the other hand to coil your lasso or rope a calf," Frank explained. "If you lean with your knees, then you can use both hands for working while riding. The horse will obey that signal for a turn."

Jack could not do it. Each time he tried, Star stopped and looked over her shoulder. *Is she laughing?* Jack wondered. Finally, he understood what he was doing and began having fun riding. *"Amazing," he thought proudly. "I can really do it."*

They took a break after about an hour, and then Frank saddled his horse to ride with Jack out into the countryside.

"Can I come?" Ann asked, brushing an unruly lock of red hair from her face.

"Not this time," Frank said. "You're too much of a distraction with that giggling of yours." Ann made a face at him, turned her back and walked away.

For the next two hours they rode through the country. Frank made the horses trot, canter, and gallop—Jack had to hold onto the saddle horn so he would not fall off— until Jack's backside ached so bad he was willing to walk back to the ranch.

When they arrived at the stables, they brushed down the horses, washed up, and went to lunch. Frank said he would teach Jack how to rope after lunch. Jack wasn't sure how he could rope anything, much less stand or walk. All he wanted to do was to go to bed.

The lunch was filled with Ann's laughter as she told everyone about Jack's problems learning to ride. He was happy when it was over. He followed Frank back to the corral. Frank got out a sawhorse with horns nailed to it. Then he gave Jack a lariat and told him to rope the "doggie." Jack threw the rope over his head as he had seen them do in the movies and succeeded in roping himself.

Then he heard that darned laugh and knew Ann was watching. Frank took his lasso and roped the sawhorse cleanly. He showed Jack how to hold the loop just so. When he tried again the lasso ended up behind him. And so it went all afternoon. Jack did improve somewhat. At least the rope went in the general direction he was aiming. Now not only his backside hurt, but his arms had joined the party.

Eventually, Ann got tired of laughing and left. Frank went to do another chore.

Time for dinner arrived. Eating very little, Jack excused himself and went to his room to lie on the bed and think. *"If I am going to be a cowboy, I'm going to have to ignore the pain and learn to ride and rope,"* he thought, staring at the ceiling. *"Otherwise I just might as well go home right now. Ann would like that. By heaven, I'm not going to let her get the last laugh!"*

CHAPTER 6: Learning to Lasso

It was dark when Jack awoke. He looked at the clock beside his bed and saw it was four in the morning. Getting out of bed quietly, he dressed and went to the barn yard to practice lassoing. It was so dark he could barely see by the light of the full moon. By five o'clock he was improving and even caught one of the horns on the "doggie." By breakfast time he was doing even better. Excited, Jack ran into the ranch house for breakfast.

"Where were you this morning?" Frank asked over his eggs and bacon.

"I went out to practice roping the 'doggie.'" He took a swallow of milk. "I roped him three out of five times."

Frank's father looked surprised. "Fine work, Jack," he said. "I knew you would get along well. Keep it up and soon you will be a good cowhand." Jack grinned at this praise and looked across the table at Ann, but she refused to look back.

"What do you think of that, 'Brighteyes'?" Jack asked Ann. "If I'm a tenderfoot, I won't be one for very long."

"Don't call me Brighteyes, Tenderfoot," Ann retorted, turned red, and then excused herself from the table.

"That was a terrible thing to call Ann," accused Rachael.

"She called Jack a tenderfoot dude first!" exclaimed Austin, ready to start a sibling fight.

"Now children." Grandpa got up and poked around at the fire. "If we are going to fight I think I should stop the story for tonight."

"No, grandpa!" the children said almost in unison.

"Please keep telling us the story," said Rachael.

"Yes, we'll be quiet," added Austin.

"Well. All right." Grandpa said. "Where were we?"

"Ann had just excused herself from the table," Rachael said.

After breakfast, Frank had Jack saddle Star. This time he didn't let the horse fool him by holding its breath. He did not want a repeat of yesterday. He could still hear Ann's laugh. In the corral Frank set up some barrels. Jack was to ride around them, steering with the reins in one hand. When he accidentally dropped them, he tied them around his hand.

"No!" yelled Frank. "If you fall off your horse with the reins tied around your hand, the horse may drag you all over the place."

Jack untied the reins from his hand, feeling foolish. *"I should have figured that out myself,"* he thought, angry with himself. He knocked over several barrels, but at least he improved. Frank and he went riding for two hours and this time Jack felt more comfortable, almost confident, but it was still painful. At lunch, Mrs. Rollin suggested that a long soak in the bathtub later would be helpful. Ann giggled.

After lunch they went back out to the corral.

Ann, who had been practicing, threw her lasso. It flew out and caught the "doggie" just right.

"He'll never do that," came Ann's sarcastic voice as she went to retrieve her rope. Jack reached up and pulled his lasso down off the saddle. He threw it at the target and also hit it just right. He leaned over to pick the rope up, but before he could, Ann had lassoed it again.

"I see we have a contest here," Frank said with a grin. "The first one that misses looses."

They both made four successful throws. Jack had never made five straight in a row. Ann threw and missed. "Brighteyes looses!" Jack yelled in excitement.

"Not yet," Frank said. "You have to throw your lasso an equal amount of times." Jack mumbled something about changing the rules and then made his throw. He wasn't even close.

"It's a tie," Frank said laughing. "But you are doing much better from the ground. Now let's try it from horseback."

Jack saddled his horse and returned to the corral. On his first attempts, he lassoed Star's head, her tail and the fence post. *"What a disaster,"* he thought. He noticed the lack of giggling and laughter from Ann, who was standing outside the corral fence watching. Soon Frank and Ann left in different directions.

Jack kept trying until his arm felt like it was about to fall off. Not caring anymore, he threw a lazy light throw and, to his great astonishment, it landed right over the horns. *"Maybe I've been trying too hard."* He attempted another light throw and succeeded again—and again.

Jack told no one of this accomplishment and took Star into the stall to unsaddle her. When he was beginning to brush the horse, Jack noticed an African-American cowhand pouring grain into the horse's feeding trough.

"I knew you'd get the knack of that lasso," said the middle aged man, who came over grinning. He was wearing faded jeans and a red checkered shirt with sleeves rolled up to the elbows. His boots were muddy and he smelled like horses.

"Sorry, I've met so many people these last few days, I forgot your name." Jack looked up at this tall cowboy. His face was dark as ebony, his hair was short cut and graying, and his eyes were jet black. But his main features were his smile and the gentleness in his tone.

"My name is Jimmy, but no matter," he said, spitting a string of tobacco juice into the straw covering the floor.

"You're learning just fine. Star is a good horse, but the other one in your string is a little frisky. I know 'cause I broke them."

"You break horses?" Jack asked with admiration.

"Sure do. Been doing it since I can remember. Star and Kicker are fine horses, but you have to control them with a steady hand, especially Kicker. The best way to start with any horse is to talk gentle and rub your hand all over them before you saddle up. Might talk some more to Star. Horses like that." He reached out and rubbed Star's neck. "Don't ya, girl?" The horse gave a snicker and nodded her head.

Jack rubbed Star between the ears, where she liked it best.

"If you ever need to know anything about horses, just ask me," Jimmy said as he went over and poured grain into Star's feed trough. Star snickered and started walking toward her stall.

"Ready to eat now?" Jack asked her softly, feeling kind of funny talking to a horse. "Thank you for your patience with me today. You deserve a good dinner." Then he led her into the stall and took the bridle off, remembering to hang it on the nail just outside. Jack's stomach rumbled and he realized that if he didn't hurry he would be late for dinner.

CHAPTER SEVEN: Roping Chickens

"Roping what?" asked Austin. He sat near the fire, intently watching a marshmallow on a stick as if it might run away as he cooked it.

As usual the kids and their grandpa had gathered around their fire pit for an evening of s'mores and listening to grandpa tell his story of Jack.

Grandpa just held up two fingers to his lips in answer to Austin's question, and Austin knew he had to be quiet.

Dinner that night was a solemn affair. Buddy had returned with bad news. More unbranded cattle had disappeared.

"We need to brand the cattle now," Frank urged, looking

at his father over a cup of coffee.

"That won't do. We would just have to have another round up later. No." He was silent a minute while he cut and ate a piece of roast beef. "We have to discover what is happening. We need proof of rustling."

"I agree, Mr. Rollin," Buddy said. "It's certainly not the ghost," he laughed.

"If you get good enough," Mr. Rollin turned to Jack, "you can come help with the branding."

"He's doing very well," said Frank. "He is beginning to ride well, and he can rope the 'doggie' from the ground."

"I bet he couldn't lasso a chicken if he tried," teased Ann, brushing a wayward lock of hair out of her eye.

"Just give me a few more days, and I'll show you, Brighteyes," Jack said, buttering a hot homemade dinner roll.

When he went to bed that night after a long hot bath, Jack was very tired and every muscle ached. *"I didn't know roping and riding could be so painful,"* he groaned as he turned over in bed. He promised himself he'd do better in the morning. *"I'll show Ann who can rope a chicken,"* he thought.

Jack slept through the night without dreaming. It was Frank's calling and shaking him that got him up. The aches and pains were even worse this morning. He could barely move. Jack dressed and went to breakfast.

"All right, Tenderfoot," Ann said. "Let's see how you do with moving targets."

"You show me the target, Brighteyes, and I'll lasso it," Jack bragged while putting a forkful of home fries, covered with catsup, into his mouth.

"Don't call me Brighteyes!" Ann demanded. "Meet me in the barnyard after breakfast and we'll see."

Jack looked at Frank who just grinned back. After breakfast, the three of them went to the barnyard, lassos in hand.

"What the heck are we going to do here, Brighteyes?" Jack asked with a grin.

"We are going to lasso chickens, Tenderfoot," Ann retorted. "The one that gets the most chickens wins."

This did not sound too hard to Jack. In the fenced yard were two dozen chickens pecking at the ground.

"I'll be the judge," Frank said. "Here are the rules: First, you must sit on the fence as if you are riding a horse. Second, the person who lassos the most hens in fifteen minutes wins. And third, I'll be the sole judge and my decision is final," he added, trying to keep from laughing.

Ann and Jack mounted the fence, but the chickens were too far away. "How are we going to lasso chickens way over there?" Ann asked as she coiled her lasso. Frank went over and started herding the chickens toward the fence.

They threw their lassos together and succeeded in tangling them up. After getting untangled, Jack threw and missed. Ann threw and caught one. Frank let the chicken go. Jack threw again, this time telling himself to relax, and caught one. After fifteen minutes of this chaos, in the midst of flying feathers and dust, Ann had lassoed five and Jack only four of the noisy, feathery birds. Jack was very depressed as he knew he would never hear the end of this from Ann.

"Another tie," Frank declared.

"A tie!" Ann was shocked. "What do you mean a tie?"

"Wait a minute Grandpa!" exclaimed Rachael. "Ann roped five chickens and Jack only got four. She has to win, doesn't she?"

"That's what she thought," Grandpa said. "But there must have been extenuating circumstances."

"What 'extenuating circumstances'?" Rachael asked with a shake of her blond hair.

"You'll see." Grandpa continued his story.

"I won, fair and square Frank!" Ann dismounted the fence and turned red with anger.

"Do you remember what I said? The one who lassos the most hens wins, but you lassoed a rooster. So you both got four hens. It's a tie."

The rest of the week involved more riding and practice roping. But things changed when Saturday morning arrived. Jack was still sore all over, but he was happy with the way he was improving. Ann seemed not to tease as much, and Jack was looking forward to riding the fence. After breakfast, Frank took Jack out and they saddled the horses. Before mounting, Frank opened a locked steel cabinet and came back with two pistols and holsters.

"You'll need to know how to shoot. You may have to use this ridin' fence."

"In case I find the rustlers?" Jack asked, wide eyed. He knew nothing about hand guns. His parents had not even let him have a BB gun.

"No. For rattlesnakes and wildcats." Frank busied himself strapping on his gun.

Jack gulped. *"I hadn't planned on rattlesnakes and wildcats. Maybe I'd better"*...His thought was interrupted by Frank, who showed him how to put the holster and six-shooter on. Frank checked the pistols to make sure they were not loaded.

"Don't worry," he said as he handed the gun to Jack. It's not loaded." He stuffed a box of cartridges in his pocket. "Let's go."

They rode for about a half an hour. Jack visualized snakes and mountain lions all the way to a ravine north of the ranch house. After dismounting, Jack looked around for a place to tie up Star.

"Just let her reins drop down," Frank instructed. "She's trained to stay put."

Sitting on a rock, Frank showed him the pistol. It was a .22 caliber six-shooter. He loaded five shells into the gun.

"We only use five shells," he explained, "and leave the hammer on the empty cylinder. This way we don't shoot ourselves. It also means you have to turn the barrel once, or pull the trigger once, before you can fire the first round."

Jack nervously loaded five rounds into the cylinder, closed it, and put it into the holster strapped to his leg. Frank set up five rocks on a dirt ledge about ten feet away. Then he pulled his pistol and shot five times. He only hit two of the rocks.

"I'm a little rusty," he said, embarrassed. "You don't have to aim, just point your pistol like a finger. You try it."

He pointed the gun and pulled the trigger. Nothing happened. Then Jack remembered the empty cylinder. He pointed a second time and the gun went off, but he had his eyes closed and did not see were the bullet went.

"Try to aim for the targets, not the top of the ravine," Frank said, laughing. "Keep your eyes open and your hand steady."

His next shots came a little closer. They continued to practice until the ammunition ran out. Frank had improved and was hitting three rocks out of five shots every time. Jack would get one and sometimes two rocks in one load of the pistol. He felt bad, not being able to do better. Frank laid a hand on Jack's shoulder.

"You didn't do too badly for the first try," he consoled, placing his pistol into its holder. "After all, I've been shooting for ten years and should have done much better. We'll try again another time. Now, let's get back and clean these weapons before supper."

After supper that night, Mr. Rollin packed them into the ranch station wagon and headed for Bluff, the only town within twenty miles. Jack was amazed to see such a small town. The highway served as the main street and there was only one intersection. At this crossing there was a gas station, a small grocery store, a drug store and a dusty sign proclaiming The Lone Star Restaurant. Next to the restaurant was a general store. "BLUFF NOTIONS," the sign on the front proclaimed.

"I thought we were going to a movie?" questioned Jack, wondering if he would have noticed the town at all if the car had been going faster.

"It only has a population of 476," said Mr. Rollin. "The movies are shown in the restaurant at seven thirty."

Mr. Rollin parked the car by the general store. Ann, Jack and Frank wandered around the town. They saw the movie, which impressed none of them.

After the movie, Ann and Jack went into the general store and browsed. Ann tried to get Jack to try on a fifteen gallon hat.

"You would look good in it, since your head seems to have grown very large," Ann teased.

"It being such a tall hat, it would make me look taller at least," Jack replied and tried on the old fashioned cowboy hat, then looked in the mirror. He looked so ridiculous that they both started laughing. In fact, he enjoyed spending the evening with her.

Later Ann stopped to look at some jewelry.

"See that necklace over there," she pointed to a necklace with a Star of Texas outlined by some sparkly jewels. "I really like that, but it's too expensive."

Jack stopped and bought a cardboard box of cinnamon Chiclets. He wanted to chew like the other cowboys, but just the thought of chewing tobacco made him sick at his stomach.

It surprised him that he and Ann had so much fun together.

Sunday the family, with Jack in tow, went to church at an old little mission just south of Bluff. Ann wore a blue dress and, Jack thought that for the first time, she looked like a girl. He smiled to himself, thinking about Ann as a young woman.

"Aw, come on Grandpa." Austin complained. "Can we stop with the girl thing? Girls stink!"

"They do not!" Rachael exclaimed. She got up, took another marshmallow, and fixed it on her stick . "I don't stink!"

"Okay kids. That's enough. Austin, some day you'll see girls in a different light." He took the toasted marshmallow that Rachael offered him. "Let's get back to the story. You'll have to go to bed in a few minutes. Perhaps we can go for a few minutes more,"

That night, Jack had some difficulty going to sleep. He

was happy Frank was going with him this first time but there were still many questions bouncing around in his mind. *Was he really capable of ridin' fence? What about snakes?* He kept switching between excitement and anxiety about his first real work as a cowboy. One great worry hovered over him as he tossed and turned. What if he came upon a wild cat? What if he shot and missed it with all five rounds! A shiver went up his spine. There was more to being a cowboy than Jack had imagined.

"Okay, that's enough for tonight. Let's clean up. Want to continue tomorrow night?"

"Oh, please, grandpa," Rachael said as she came over to give him a hug.

"It depends whether you are going to keep on with this girl stuff," Austin said as he picked up some trash and took it in with him.

CHAPTER EIGHT: Ridin' Fence

Jack could hardly control his excitement. Breakfast was gobbled so fast that Mrs. Rollin told him to slow down.

"Those fences will still be there after breakfast. Besides," she continued, "you'll need food to give you energy."

"She's right," Frank said as he grabbed another piece of thick homemade toasted bread. "Eat up."

Jack tried hard for self-control. Today he would really become a cowboy and ride fence. He forced another piece of toast, smothered with butter and strawberry jam, into his mouth.

After what seemed like an eternity, he and Frank went to the stables where Frank handed him chaps and then some metal objects.

"What are these?" Jack questioned.

"Spurs," replied Frank. "They go on your boots and help you control your horse."

Jack looked at the spurs, but they did not look like the spurs he had seen cowboys wear in the movies.

"I thought spurs had round sharp things on them."

"Mine do." He pointed to his spurs. "However, you don't know how to use them and you might hurt your horse. You start with these training spurs," Frank explained, pointing to the ends of the spurs. "See the round knobs at the end? They can't hurt a horse if misused, yet they will help in controlling him. On this ranch you have to earn your real spurs by showing you can handle a horse without them."

Frank showed Jack how to attach the spurs to his boots. Then they saddled the horses, packed some tools and sandwiches into saddle bags, and started out. They rode side by side for a while.

As they trotted along Frank said, "Ridin' fence is a very important part of ranching. What we are going to do is look for broken fences and bad spots in the barbed wire. If the fence is broken then cattle will escape and we lose money."

A few minutes later, Frank turned and added, "We also need to see if anyone has cut the fence and rustled our cattle. I wish I knew what was happening—how we are losing cattle, I mean. Anyway, keep your eyes open."

Soon they had to go single file along a trail which paralleled the fence. The fence was made of barbed wire strung in four strands on posts about twelve feet apart. The wire was rusty in some places and new in others. Jack pointed this out to Frank.

"It would cost too much to try to replace several hundreds of miles of wire at the same time, so we just replace those parts that have broken or which are in very bad shape."

"Hundreds of miles of wire?" he asked, incredulous.

"Well, for every mile of fence there are four miles of wire. The perimeter fences are about forty miles in length and four strands for each mile, so that's one hundred-sixty miles of barbed wire. I can't guess how much fence separates the pastures."

"You mean we have to ride forty miles today?" Jack asked, already feeling pain in his backside.

"Not that far, thank goodness," Frank smiled. "We'll ride about twenty miles today to the back bunkhouse, spend the night there and tomorrow ride another twenty miles back to the ranch house."

Jack stood in his stirrups to relieve the pain he was already feeling. "Oh my aching backside."

"You don't know the half of it. But you will by tonight, and tomorrow night you will know the whole of it!" Frank laughed and picked up the pace. "We got to get a move on if we're going to make the bunk house by dark."

As the day wore on it got hot, and no matter how Jack sat on the saddle his butt hurt. The fence line ran up low hills, across stream beds, over gullies, and across flat hot plains. He only saw a few cattle.

"Where are all the cattle?"

"Oh, they're smarter than we are. Most have found some

shade near a source of water and are resting while we're out in the sun riding our buns off."

They stopped at noon to eat lunch and sat on a large rock that stuck out from a low cliff. Jack noticed that Frank looked all around the rock before sitting down.

"Snakes," was all he said.

Jack examined every crevice and around the rock.

"It's all right," Frank said with a laugh. "I checked."

"I don't like snakes," Jack said nervously. "I don't like them at all."

After giving one last look around Jack sat down, easing his sore backside onto the stone. The coolness of the shade washed over him. Suddenly he discovered he was starving. He rummaged around in the saddle bag and pulled out the huge sandwiches Frank's mother had made. One was roast beef and the other was ham and cheese. Each sandwich, wrapped in brown paper, seemed to weigh a pound, but Jack found he was able to eat both of them plus the potato chips and a generous slice of apple pie. They washed down the food with cool water from their canteens.

"Don't move," Frank said quietly. He was standing to stretch his legs.

"What!" shouted Jack, knowing there must be a snake nearby.

"Be quiet and don't move. There is a big scorpion next to your leg."

Jack, unable to control himself, jumped. At the same

time, Frank brushed the scorpion away with his hat.

"That thing is almost two inches long," Jack said, shaking from the scare.

"Yep. It's a big 'en. The big ones hurt when they strike, but it's the little ones that will kill you."

"That's it," Rachael said. "I don't want to be a cowgirl. It's bad enough with snakes, but bugs that will kill you—no way!"

"You're just a sissy," chided Austin. "They wouldn't bother me. Not unless they came near," he said, laughing.

"Well I don't like the thoughts of snakes or scorpions...or mountain lions either," Grandpa added. "But that was all part of a cowboy's life then." He turned to Austin, "Please put some more wood on the fire. It's getting cold. While you're doing that, I'll continue the story."

After Jack settled down, they watered the horses by pouring water into their hats and letting the horses drink. Then they tightened the cinches and mounted. Jack noticed Frank pour some of the water from the canteen over his head before he put his hat back on.

"Keeps you cooler in this heat," he said, nudging his horse onto the path. Jack copied Frank and hurried to catch up.

An hour later, Frank drew up his horse and dismounted.

Jack got off Star, wondering why they had stopped.

He walked over to the fence. "The top wire is broken and the other three don't look too good either. Might have been deer jumping the fence." He looked at the barbs of the broken wire. "See, here is some hair they left behind. Probably being chased by coyotes."

Frank reached for the coil of wire on his saddle. Jack got the wire cutters and pliers out of his saddle bag.

"Time for you to learn how to make a temporary repair," Frank said.

After pulling on some leather gloves, he cut a piece of new wire. Then, using the pliers, he attached it to the broken wire about a foot from the break. On the other side he made a loop, threaded the new wire through and pulled it tight. Winding the new wire about itself, he cut it. Then he pulled out a notebook.

"We need to remember to tell them at the bunkhouse where this break is."

Jack looked around. "How do we know where the break is?"

"It's no mystery," Frank said, and walked over to the nearest post, shook his head and walked to the next one. "Come here," he said, pointing.

Walking over to the post, Jack saw that at the bottom of the post there was a steel tag with a number nailed on it. It was hard to see and Frank had to scrape it with his knife, but there was the number 153.

"So all we have to do is tell them that it's near post 153. Every other post is supposed to be numbered, but sometimes they rust off."

Late in the afternoon, they came to a small creek. They let the horses drink while munching on apples and swilling water from their second canteen.

"We've been drinking too much," Frank said, wiping his mouth with the back of his hand. "You should try never to drink from the second canteen if possible. It should be saved for emergencies only."

It was near twilight when they spotted the bunk house in the distance. It was a long rectangular building with a stable and a large corral. On one side an old Ford pick-up was parked and a stream of smoke issued from a chimney. The day had been hot, but the evening turned chilly. Frank reached back and untied his jacket from the saddle.

"It gets cool quick," Frank said. "Better put on your jacket." After some fumbling, Jack was able to don his own jacket.

Jack thought he'd never make the last mile. His butt hurt, his thighs hurt, his back hurt, and he knew he would never walk or sit again. Jack leaned to the left and then he leaned to the right in his saddle. He stood in the stirrups, but no matter what position he tried, he hurt. At last they rode into the corral and one of the hands came out to meet them.

CHAPTER NINE: The Back Bunkhouse

"**J**ack, meet Tork. He's the foreman back here," Frank said as he slid off his horse. "Tork, this is Jack. He's gonna be ridin' fence from now on."

"Tork Matsen," the skinny cowhand said, stretching out his calloused right hand. After climbing unsteadily off of Star, Jack shook hands and looked into blue eyes framed by a sun burned and wrinkled face. He was a little shorter than six feet tall and about as blond as one can get.

"Heard you was comin'. Welcome to the back bunkhouse." He turned to Frank. "Any problems?"

Frank, who was taking the saddle off his horse, told Tork of the broken fence. When he finished, he disappeared into the stable with his horse.

Jack gave a low groan as he started to take the saddle off Star and was surprised and embarrassed when Tork came over to help.

"Don't worry," Tork said with a grin. "I still remember my first long ride. I looked like a duck when I walked."

"I'm not sure I can walk at all," Jack confessed.

Tork let out a loud guffaw and said, "Don't ya worry. We'll have your dinner set up on the fireplace mantle so ya can stand and eat." He chuckled as he carried Jack's saddle into the stable. Jack led Star into the stable and brushed her down prior to putting her into an empty stall. Before he left, he made sure there was water, hay and grain.

"At least it's good to know you've been trained well in how to care for your horse," Tork said.

"Well, Frank trained me," he said, feeling proud of himself.

"Frank is a good man," Tork said, "and he'll be a good rancher, too."

They entered the bunk house together and Jack was greeted by the commotion of ten men eating and the smell of tobacco mixed with the lush smell of stew. His mouth started to water. Seeing him enter, there was sudden quiet.

"This is Jack," Tork said and walked over to a place at the table.

Various men seated at the long table greeted him with smiles as he limped into the room.

"Well, what's wrong with you kid? Never learn to walk

right?" one guy, skinny with black unruly hair, asked. Everyone laughed.

"Leave the kid alone, Jed!" the cook yelled as he straightened up from his stove in the cooking alcove.

"Now Pete," said another, "he surely does walk funny. I wonder how he sits?"

"Don't worry about sitting," Tork said, "I've laid a place for him over on the mantle of the fireplace." There was more laughter and Jack knew his face must be so red it glowed even in the well lit bunk house.

Jack looked at the fireplace and sure enough a place had been set there.

"Now boys," Pete said, "let the poor guy alone." He came over to Jack and led him to a place at the table. Jack sat down as gently as possible.

"Perhaps . . . I could borrow a pillow."

The room resounded with guffaws and laughter over his remark, but at least they seemed to be laughing with him and not just at him. Jack knew he'd never walk right again.

"Why were the men so mean?" asked Rachael.

"They weren't really being mean. Cowboys tease one another a lot. In their way they were welcoming me into their family, but I must admit I didn't know it at the time." Grandpa shifted in his chair, then continued.

Frank had joined some men at the other end of the table and during dinner everyone laughed and talked as they ate.

Pete placed a large plate of steaming beef stew and a stack of homemade bread in front of him.

"Dig in," he commanded, walking back to the alcove where his beloved stove, upon which many pots were bubbling, took almost the whole wall. It was a kitchen like none other Jack had seen.

Jack looked around the chow hall as he ate. The room was large enough to accommodate four times as many men. There were four long tables that ran the length of the room, but only one of them was in use tonight. Between the huge spoonfuls of stew, he saw that the walls were made of knotty pine planks which shone from many coats of varnish. Here and there on the walls were framed rodeo posters. On one wall was a pin-up calendar which Jack thought he would like to get a better look at.

He swiped a slab of butter over a piece of bread and took a large bite. He noticed, as he chewed, that over the entryway were three mounted stag deer heads and, on either side of the door, a line of pegs was set into the wall. Coats and cowboy hats hung on them.

Jack took another spoonful of stew and discovered he was chewing on a piece of gristle. Not knowing what else to do, he turned his head and swallowed it with a gulp. He continued to survey the room and saw a huge fireplace with a few battered stuffed chairs and an old sofa facing it. The lighting in the room was provided by four large wagon wheel lamps hanging from the rafters. A cozy place, Jack thought as he took another bite of homemade bread.

"Hey, Cookie," shouted one of the men. "Better bring more stew. This young whippersnapper needs fattening."

"Don't mind the teasing," said Tork, who was sitting beside him. "All newcomers get the same treatment." He took a mouthful of stew and followed it with a slug of coffee. "You doing all right?" he questioned, looking serious, his blue eyes focused on Jack.

"Yeah, I'm doing all right, but I ache all over." Jack buttered another hunk of the fresh bread and scooped up some gravy from the stew. He was famished. "How long have you been a cowboy?"

"Since I was a kid. My father jumped ship in Galveston in the twenties. He was only sixteen but he knew one thing. He didn't want to be a sailor. He changed his name from Ultermatsen to Matsen and I'm happy he did."

"Why is that?" Jack was interested in Tork's story, as it took his mind off the throbbing pain in his thighs and bottom.

"So I didn't have to learn how to spell it," Tork grinned. "It was too dang long. Matsen is good enough for me. Anyway, he found himself a job as a wrangler and worked for several ranches in Texas. He met my mother in San Antonio, got drunk and married her, and soon I appeared. That changed his life."

"It changed his life?" Jack asked, taking another mouthful of the thick stew.

"Sure did. With a wife and me, he had to settle down.

Became a foreman for the Double Bar Ranch north of here. It was only natural for me to take to cowpokin' as a young boy. It's a tough life but I love the outdoors and the friendship."

Pete placed a large bowl of banana pudding in front of Jack. "Made this special for you. It's a favorite dessert with the hands. Eat up!" He took away Jack's empty plate and came back to watch him eat. Jack knew immediately he did not like the pudding, because he hated bananas. He also knew he would have to eat it all or Pete's feelings would be hurt.

"I'll show you your bunk," Pete said later, after Jack had struggled through the last bite.

"I guess I'm pretty tired," Jack said, getting up slowly and painfully. Pete showed him the bunk where he was to sleep. Someone had put his saddle bags on the bed.

"The shower is through that door," Pete said pointing at a door at the far end of the large room lined with double bunks. There was space for forty hands, Jack thought. He knew there were not more than ten men here and only the lower bunks appeared to be occupied.

Noticing Jack's curiosity Pete said, "We only fill this place when there is a round up. Then we are very crowded and busy." He handed Jack a bottle. "Rub some of this on your sore spots. It will take the pain away." Pete said good night and went back into the chow hall. Jack looked at the label on the brown bottle: "Dr. Jaren's Horse Liniment." Well, Jack guessed, even horses have pains.

The hot shower felt good on his back and neck. He took a long time letting it massage his backside. When he got out, he rubbed a little of Dr. Jaren's Liniment on his thighs, expecting it to hurt or something. It smelled funny and he wondered if this was just another joke. He continued to rub the stuff all over his back and legs, put on his pajamas and climbed into his bunk. He had hardly pulled up the covers when it began to burn. He thought about getting into the shower and trying to wash it off, but before he made that decision, he was fast asleep.

CHAPTER TEN: Kicker

They had been riding for an hour now, and Jack was still struggling to control Kicker, the second horse of his string. Getting up before dawn was bad, but having to eat all the food Pete made for breakfast was worse. After eating, Jack had gone to the stable to get Star saddled.

"Wait a minute," Frank said, coming in. "You're riding Kicker today. Star gets to rest until you come back."

"What? Star gets to rest but I have to work?" Jack said with indignation. He was still feeling the pain from the night before, but it was not as bad this morning. Perhaps the liniment had worked some after all. He was glad he had stuffed it into the saddle bag.

Jack brought Kicker out of the stall without much trouble. He was black as midnight with a white diamond on his forehead. There was a patch of white also on his chest and it looked as if he was wearing white socks. As he saddled the horse he talked to him, just as he had been taught. But when he tried to mount him he sidled around and went in circles until Frank caught and steadied the reins.

Right after Jack got settled in the saddle, Kicker stood on his hind legs. Jack flew through the air and landed in the dirt on his already sore backside.

"You all right?" Frank asked, looking him over.

"I think so," Jack replied tentatively, checking out his body parts.

"Go t to be careful with Kicker." He helped Jack up from the ground. "He needs to know you're the boss. So get back up and make him behave. If you have to, give him a little kick with your spurs."

Jack went over to the horse, which shied away from him again until he caught the reins. Looking Kicker in the eye he said in a stern voice, "I'm the boss Mr. Kicker, and I don't like to be thrown. Now you behave!" As he mounted, Kicker tried the circle stunt again, making it hard to mount. When he finally was firmly seated for the second time, he gave him a light kick with his dull spurs, and to his great surprise the horse obeyed him. But after an hour of riding, Jack thought Kicker might be biding his time, waiting for a good place, like a cactus patch, to throw him.

This side of the ranch was a wilder place. There were more hills and deep ravines he had to negotiate. He was happy to have Frank along to show him the trails. As they walked and led their horses back up one steep ravine, Frank stopped suddenly.

"Don't move," he said in a low voice as he slowly drew his pistol. Jack heard the click as the barrel was turned to a live round.

"What is it?" Jack whispered, looking around. He could see nothing.

"A rattlesnake in the path ahead."

Jack looked again and, after a few seconds, was able to focus and see the snake. It was almost camouflaged by its coloring. He felt a little sick and a lot like running back down the trail.

"Blam, Blam, Blam!," Frank's pistol spoke with authority. Spouts of dust and rock flew up around the snake, which slithered quickly over the ledge and out of sight.

"Did you kill him?" Jack wanted to know, because he didn't want to pass the place with a live rattlesnake hiding somewhere waiting for him.

"Don't think so," Frank said, reloading and holstering his six-shooter as he started on up the trail. "These snakes like to make nests in the cracks in the rocks. Its cool in the heat of the day and the trail is warm at night."

"Then what's the darned thing doing on the trail this late in the morning?" Jack asked, eyes swiveling in search of more snakes.

"Oh," said Frank, looking over his shoulder and laughing. "He was just sunbathing, I guess."

"I don't think I want to go any farther," Jack said,

attempting to turn Kicker around on the narrow trail.

"Come on Jack," Frank urged. "Just keep your eyes open. Normally they won't bother you unless you or your horse gets too near."

Sweating profusely, Jack followed Frank, his eyes darting from ledges to cracks in the rocks. When they got to the top of the ravine, they remounted and Frank asked Jack to take the lead. "Don't forget to keep your eye on the fence and look for breaks. We should also look out for any signs of rustlers."

"What kinds of signs?"

"Oh, a broken fence, or a just repaired fence with tire tracks, or a lot of cattle tracks," Frank said, shifting on the saddle and patting his holster.

"How am I supposed to keep my eye on the fence . . . and on the trail . . . and look out for snakes at the same time?" Jack mumbled, still frightened. He nudged Kicker into motion.

At noon they rested by a trickle of water in a creek bed where the horses could drink their fill. An old stunted tree provided shade as they ate the lunch Pete had fixed for them. Jack looked around and saw some distant hills and mountains. A few clouds drifted in a deep blue sky. Closer to them, at the bottom of the hill, was a small valley filled with cactus and sage brush.

"Gosh it's beautiful!" Jack exclaimed. "What are those mountains over there?"

"They're part of the Big Bend National Park," Frank said,

"and they are about one hundred miles from here."

"They sure don't look that far."

After lunch, Jack again took the lead and they continued along the fence line. At three in the afternoon they stopped to rest in the shade of a large boulder. Near exhaustion, Jack leaned back on the cool rock and closed his eyes. He must have fallen asleep, because the next thing he knew Frank was shaking him.

"Come look at this," Frank said as he walked around the rock. He pointed to a sandy place between two rocks.

"What?" Jack rubbed the sleep from his eyes.

"Don't you see that print?"

Jack bent over and looked into the sand. There was a paw print. "What kind of animal made this track?"

"It's a mountain lion. Must live somewhere around here or at least hunt near here."

Jack looked all around and, not seeing an animal lurking in the rocks, bent over to look at the print closely. It was about an inch and a half in diameter and had four toes around a pad.

"I think it was a medium sized cat as they come. I once saw a print that was more than two inches in diameter," Frank said, squatting down. "See how it points a little to the right? That is most likely his right front paw. He was running along the trail and made a leap past these stones, just touching the ground with his paw. I'll bet if we follow his tracks we'll find the remains of the prey he was after." Frank looked up at Jack, his eyes inviting him to follow the track.

"No th...tha...thanks," Jack stuttered, "We better get going or we'll not get in before dark."

"You're right," Frank sighed, mounting his horse.

They reached the ranch just before sundown. Mrs. Rollin and Ann were there to meet them. "Come along and have a wash," said Mrs. Rollin. "It's almost dinner time."

They took the horses into the stable with Ann following and asking a hundred questions.

"Was it hard? Did you see any wildcats? Did you find tracks of the rustlers?" the questions poured out without giving them time to answer.

Jack was much too tired and hungry to answer her with anything but a mumbled "Later. Let's talk later."

He was thankful when Jimmy came and took their horses.

"You both look beat," he said. "Let me take care of the horses for you."

Jack and Frank went to their rooms and tossed a coin to see who got the first shower. Frank won.

"That's enough for tonight kids," grandpa said, struggling to arise from his chair. Austin came over and gave him a helping hand. "We can continue tomorrow."

"I'll put out the fire," Rachael said. "You can take the marshmallows in, Austin."

"Awe, you can do that too. I made the fire."

Grandpa went into the house, never knowing who won.

INTERLUDE: Grandpa

All day the rain had been beating on the windows, and Rachael and Austin were restless from not being able to go outside. After dinner they began to argue about who was going to clear the table, whose turn it was to fill the dish washer, and what TV show they wanted to watch. Everything that came up seemed to cause them to argue.

"All right, children," their grandfather said. "I'm tired of this arguing over everything. What is the problem, anyway?"

"We're tired of the rain," Austin said, his eyes down.

"Yeah," added Rachael, "and we can't go out and have a campfire tonight. I was looking forward to more som'mores, grandpa."

"Why don't we light a fire in the fireplace and at least have a cup of hot chocolate," grandpa suggested.

"But we don't have fires inside during the summer," Austin said.

"I think it will be all right tonight. It'll take the dampness out of the air."

"I'll make the cocoa," said Rachael.

"Grandpa, can I make the fire in the fire place?"

It didn't take long before there was a nice fire going and everyone sat down. Grandpa sat in his special chair, Austin was on the sofa, and Rachael curled next to her lamb stool that had been hers since she was born.

"Can we continue with the cowboy story?"

"Tenderfoot dude, stupid," Austin growled.

"We'll have an early bedtime if you two don't stop snapping at each other."

"We'll be good, Grandpa," Rachael said with a side look at Austin, who nodded his head.

Grandpa sat back in his chair and scratched his beard, "Where was I last time..."

"I want to know more about Ann," said Rachael.

"Brighteyes!" interrupted Austin.

Grandpa looked at Austin with what was known as his "I'm about the end of my rope" look.

Austin slumped down on the couch, evidently understanding the warning.

"What do you want to know about her?" asked Grandpa.

"What she is thinking? How does she feel about being called Brighteyes? Why does she give Jack such a bad time? Stuff like that."

"I have no idea of what was really going on in her mind, or at least I didn't at the time. I suppose I could guess now, but all it would be is a guess."

"That's OK, Grandpa. Go ahead."

The grandfather took a sip of his chocolate, stared into the distance for a minute and looked sad. Then he took a deep breath and brightened up.

CHAPTER ELEVEN: Ann

While Frank and Jack were gone, Ann had many feelings to sort out. She had started to like the dark haired, hazel-eyed boy who was trying so hard to be a cowboy. She felt sorry for the way she had laughed at him every time he did something wrong. When she was learning she had made as many mistakes as Jack had, but nobody had laughed at her. Sure she was teased a little, but not laughed at.

Why had she reacted to him this way? She tried to figure it out but was not able to. One thing she knew for sure: he was not a coward. When he fell he got up again, and when there was something to learn he worked hard to learn it. Ann knew she had to apologize somehow, and had to do it soon. Until then she had to control her tongue and laughter.

She put on a pretty skirt and blouse, made sure her hair

was right, and then headed for the dining room. On the way Mrs. Rollin stopped her.

"You sure are dressed up tonight." Mrs. Rollin stood back to get a better look at Ann in her finery.

"I just thought it would be nice to dress up a little," Ann said as a blush spread over her cheeks.

"Oh," said Mrs. Rollin, "I thought maybe it was because Jack was here tonight." Mrs. Rollin chuckled and headed to the kitchen for more food before Ann could say anything. The blush on Ann's face became a deeper hue of red, and the more she attempted to control it the hotter her face felt. *Had she dressed up for Jack? Maybe so.*

Jack and Frank were already there when Ann arrived. She saw Jack gulp when she entered. That was when she was sure she had dressed up for Jack. She wanted to impress him as a girl, not the silly brat she had been the first week.

"Hi," she said to Jack, "You look good tonight."

"Thanks," Jack replied. "So do you." He looked down in his lap.

Was he blushing? Ann wasn't sure. Throughout dinner she said little to him, but watched him out of the corner of her eye.

During dessert, Mr. Rollin asked Frank how the fence riding went.

"Very good, dad," Frank said. "Jack did fine, although he has a few aches and pains."

Jack waited for Ann's laughter and was surprised when

she just looked at him.

"We didn't have but one break down by post 153. There is a twenty foot section of the fence that needs replacing." Frank added, "We saw no signs of rustlers anywhere along the fence."

Mr. Rollin looked at Jack and smiled. "Think you can ride fence by yourself day after tomorrow?"

Jack returned the look and felt his heart thumping like a herd of cattle on a stampede. Then he said as steady as he could, "I think I can do that. Sure."

"Great," Mr. Rollin said with a smile. "I knew you would be a fast learner. You can sleep in late tomorrow if you want. It's nice to have another hand."

Jack beamed with pleasure even though he was not sure how he would do the task before him. But he did know he was going to give it his best try.

Jack, Frank and Ann went into the patio after dinner.

"Do you two have time now to answer some of my questions?" she asked with a little sarcasm in her voice. Darn it all, she said to herself. I almost blew it.

"Sure," Frank replied, not seeming to notice her tone of voice. "We saw one rattler and a paw print of a wild cat. But sorry, no rustlers or outlaws."

"Was it hard, Jack? I mean for your first time ridin' fence?"

"Yes and no," Jack replied. "Yes, it was hard on my thighs and backside, but no, it was great fun. I'm looking forward to doing it by all by myself."

"What?" Frank said, "You don't need me anymore?"

Now it was Jack's turn to be embarrassed. "That's not what meant. I want to learn a lot more things about handling cattle before you go to ROTC. I still need more practice calf roping."

"Great," Frank said, "I hear they're going to do some early branding at the northwest pasture tomorrow. Want to come?"

"Sure," Jack said with enthusiasm.

"May I come also?" Ann asked.

"Why not?" Frank said. "Just be sure you wear some proper clothes for roping calves. That dress just won't do." Frank laughed. Now it was Ann's turn to be embarrassed.

Later Frank excused himself. He wanted to talk to his father about some ideas that had developed during the two day tour of the fence.

Ann and Jack sat and did not speak for a few minutes.

"Nice night," Jack said, looking up at the broad expanse of stars.

"Yes. And not too hot either," Ann said.

"That's right." Jack wondered what to say next. He did not have much experience with girls and just wanted to get away from her. But she seemed to want to talk, so he stayed.

"Jack..." Ann started.

"Yes?"

"Jack, I want to apologize for the way I have been acting. I mean my calling you a tenderfoot dude, and laughing at you.

That wasn't very nice, and I apologize."

"That's all right," he said, not really meaning it. He had been hurt badly when he fell off the horse and she laughed.

"I know I've been acting like a stupnagle since we've met," she said in a quiet voice.

"What's a 'stupnagle?'" Jack asked as he brushed an insect flying close to his ear.

"Well...it's a word that means acting like you're stupid... doing stupid things like I did."

Jack felt sorry for her and was happy she had apologized.

"I acted stupid also," he apologized. "Can we start again?"

"Oh, please, let's," Ann agreed.

"Only one thing."

"What's that?"

"Can I still call you 'Brighteyes?'"

Ann hit him on the shoulder, thought a minute and then said with a big grin, "Sure, why not? Shake on it?"

They shook hands.

"I bet I can rope more calves than you tomorrow," Ann said over her shoulder as she left the patio. "Good night."

Jack sat a few minutes longer, trying to figure girls out. Then he gave it up and headed for his bed and Dr. Jaren's Liniment.

CHAPTER TWELVE: Ropin' Calves

Ann, Jack and Frank pulled their horses up outside the branding corral in the northwest pasture. They sat watching six men hard at work. The cattle milling around inside and outside the corral made the work dusty. A fire in a pit added smoke to the dust hanging in the air. There was a narrow pen with a calf in it, and past this gate was a trough the calves were made to swim through. The cowpokes were whistling and yelling as they herded the bawling calves into the pen. The noise of the clanging doors of the holding gates in addition to the other sounds made it so loud that he wanted to cover his ears.

"What's happening?" he asked Frank.

"When we brand the cattle we try to accomplish three things," Frank explained. "Dip them for cattle ticks and other insects, inoculate them against disease, and brand them so others will know they belong to us. Those that get away and aren't branded are mavericks and anyone can claim ownership just by branding them. That is also why rustlers want to steal young unbranded cattle, although there are some who can change a brand. But that's hard work."

Frank looked at Ann and Jack. "Well, are you two ready to go to work?"

"What do we do?" Jack asked.

"See the cattle outside the fence? Those calves have not yet been branded. Your job is to pick a calf, lasso it and bring it to the branding corral."

"But there are large cows there also," Jack observed.

"Well, now Jack," Frank said, "that's what makes it interesting. You see the calves do not want to be separated from their mothers and sometimes the mothers get angry when you take their calves. So the best thing to do is to work quickly to get the calf away from the mother and over to the corral."

Frank whistled to Buddy, the ranch foreman, and hollered. "Got ya two new hands to rope some calves!" Everyone stopped what they were doing. Some laughed, others snickered. Jack wanted to run and hide. He looked at Ann who, he thought, was thinking the same thing.

"Maybe we are in over our heads," he said to Ann.

"I still bet I get more calves than you," she called over her shoulder as she galloped off toward the cattle, un-slinging her lasso from the saddle as she went.

Jack, knowing he would be unable to get his lasso ready on the run, tied an end to the saddle horn as he had been taught. Then he made sure there were no kinks in the line. Ready at last he trotted off, eyeing the herd. "Relax when you throw," he reminded himself under his breath repeatedly.

A calf darted from the compressed herd and Jack charged after it, threw his lasso and, by a stroke of pure luck, caught it around the neck. He started pulling it toward the corral when he saw Ann, who had also caught a calf, but by the foot instead of the neck. She waited while Frank straightened out the situation.

"That one doesn't count!" Jack yelled. When he reached the corral a cowpoke took the lasso and handed him another, grinning. Jack turned back to the milling cows and calves. He coughed the dust out of his throat, wiped the sweat from his face and pulled the handkerchief Frank had made him wear over his face to cut out some of the dust.

He missed the next two calves, but connected with the third. It started howling for its mother, refusing to budge. The mother, a huge beast, came out of the crowded herd and eyed him. Jack hoped the father wasn't around. He yanked on the calf, which began to follow him. After a few seconds, Jack looked behind to see how the calf was doing. His eyes opened wide when he saw the calf's mother charging him with her head down. He pulled harder on the rope to make the calf move faster. Just when the cow was about to hit him, Frank came riding by waving his hat. The cow changed direction and Jack was saved.

They broke work for lunch, sitting on the corral fence

eating sandwiches.

"How many did you get, young un?" asked a cowboy sitting beside him.

Jack looked over at the thin but wiry cowhand sitting next to him. He had an unusual profile which aroused Jack's curiosity. The man's hair was long and deep black, like midnight. It was tied in a pony tail. He had deep wrinkles in his face, a prominent nose, and around his head he wore a bright blue bandanna. Jack, tired from the work, hardly had the energy to say anything.

"Oh, by the way, they call me Begay." the cowboy continued. Jack remembered there was an Indian cowhand on the ranch by this name. He looked thirty years old or more if you measured age by the lines in his face.

"Eight," answered Jack, attracted to this strange man..

"Just eight?" he laughed, "We'll never get the branding done at that rate."

"Oh darn it," said Ann, sitting on the fence in her blue jeans and pink shirt, her calf roping outfit she had called it when Frank teased her. She pushed back a stray lock of unruly hair. "I only got five."

"Hey Begay!" another hand called derisively. "Aren't we happy to have such good help?" A few of the hands laughed.

Begay took another bite of his sandwich and gazed into the distance, chewing with deliberation. Then, still looking in the distance, distinctly and slowly, he said, "They are doing more than some paid hands at least."

"Frank," he asked later, "who was that man who called to Begay?" Jack had seen him at the back bunkhouse.

"He's new here," Frank said, "I think his name is Jed. I heard a lot of the men don't like him because of his smart mouth."

By the end of the day, Ann and Jack were working together. They more than doubled the calves caught in the morning. After dinner that evening, they sat in their favorite place in the patio, still tired from the hard work they had done, and discussed the events of the day.

"We make a great team, don't we?" Ann asked, looking at Jack intently.

"Yeah, sure, we work well together," Jack answered. "Did you see that cow try to stop me from taking her calf? I was sure happy when Frank chased her away."

They sat in quiet for a few minutes looking at the clear night sky.

"It's a little cold tonight," Jack said with a shiver.

"Are you worried about ridin' fence alone tomorrow?" Ann asked in a serious tone.

"Well..." Jack replied, wondering if he should tell what he really felt or if he should be macho. "I am a little worried, not about the ride, but mostly about snakes and wildcats."

Ann shivered and pushed that pesky, and Jack thought interesting, lock of hair from her cheek. "I don't like snakes either, but I don't think you'll have to worry about wild cats."

Jack asked if she would like to borrow his jacket. He

helped her put the jacket around her shoulders to keep her warm and told her of the paw print they had found.

"You'll do all right," Ann said, wanting to give him encouragement. She started to reach for his hand but pulled back at the last second.

"Yeah," Jack, sitting up straighter, said. "I know I can do it."

CHAPTER THIRTEEN: Wildcats, Rattlesnakes, and Scorpions

At dawn the next morning, Jack headed out from the ranch, riding Kicker again. The horse did not give him any trouble this time. He shivered in the damp cold of the morning and looked to the east, where the sun was beginning to lift over the horizon. He was not sure if he wanted it to rise. It would be very hot by noon. He stopped Kicker on the top of a low hill where his cold shivering turned into cold sweat. Jack didn't want to go on. He had to face it; he was afraid. Afraid of snakes, wild cats, and most of all, rustlers. Suppose he came upon the ghost of Cuerno de Vaca? He swallowed his fear and after several attempts nudged the horse forward. His stomach, queasy with fear, rode with him.

Kicker trotted along without event. After a couple of hours, Jack stopped by a rivulet for a break and to water his horse. Before dismounting, he spent several minutes looking all around for snakes. He slid off the horse and sat on a rock in the shade of a scrub tree. The fear subsiding, he began to relax and enjoy the ride. *Not nearly so sore today*, he thought. Jack looked at the sky filled with bleached white clouds loafing along. He reached for his handkerchief to mop the sweat off his face when he noticed something move by his leg. Leaping off the rock, Jack almost fell flat on his face. There, next to where he had been sitting, was a scorpion about two inches long. Using his red and white checked bandanna, he mopped his face, doubly wet now with fear.

He took a swig of water from his canteen, then mounted his horse and moved down the fence line, his hands shaking. Another thing to worry about, Jack thought. "Wild cats, snakes. and scorpions...Oh my!" Then he laughed.

By sundown the back bunkhouse was in sight, and he was hurting again. Jack was sure he would never be able to ride the next day. Would he ever stop hurting?

"Well, you made it!" Tork greeted him as he rode into the corral. "How'd it go?"

"Great," Jack said not sure if he meant it or not. "There were no breaks in the fence line."

He took the saddle and blanket off Kicker. He patted the horse on the rump and headed him toward the stable. Jack knew that Tork would have done this for him, but the others would surely find out and tease him for being a "kid."

"All I saw was a huge scorpion sitting next to me." He gave an involuntary shiver just thinking of the sting he had barely escaped.

"They can sting pretty bad," Tork said with sympathy in his voice. He pulled out a Bull Durham tobacco bag and rolled a cigarette with one hand. Jack had seen this done in cowboy movies, now it was being done right before his face.

"Can you teach me how to do that?" Jack asked.

"You smoke?"

"No," Jack replied, "but that is what real cowboys do, isn't it?"

"I wish I didn't smoke. Just gets in the way of things. But I don't seem to be able to stop."

"I don't want to smoke," Jack said, knowing he was about to get a sermon. "I just want to know how to roll a cigarette with one hand."

"All right," Tork laughed. "If you promise not to smoke, I'll show you how it's done. But it takes lot of practice."

They went into the bunkhouse and it seemed that the hands hardly noticed him now except for Pete, who came running over and started mothering him.

"Are you all right? Did you have any trouble?" Pete babbled, wringing his hands as he looked Jack all over,

"I'm fine," Jack insisted, forcing a smile. "Had a good day."

"You're walking as if you still hurt."

"Well, I do . . . a little," Jack admitted. "That horse liniment is a big help. I use it all the time."

"If you need more, just holler," Pete said, rubbing his hands on the stained apron he always wore. "Dinner is ready. Go wash and find a seat. We're having roast beef and peach cobbler for dessert."

Jack's mouth was watering as he scrubbed up and changed out of his dusty clothes. The dinner was wonderful and this time no one teased him. He felt that he was accepted as one of the gang. The conversation centered on the missing cattle. Nobody knew how the cattle were taken or even if they were taken.

"Maybe the cows are not birthing as much this year," suggested a cowhand named Whiley. The dark cowboy with deep set black eyes leaned back on his chair and sharpened his knife. Each time he passed the sharpening stone over the knife blade there was a long "scra...a...a...pe. And each time Jack's hair stood on end. "It could be that the grass wasn't good enough this year and the cows didn't calve." Whiley threw the knife so fast Jack did not see it leave his hand. It stuck with a "thunk" into the support beam on the far side of the chow hall.

"Yes," said Tork, ignoring Whiley who walked over to retrieve his knife. "But it's rather unlikely."

"Scra . . . a . . .a . . . p" sounded the knife as Whiley continued his sharpening.

"I wish you would stop throwing that knife inside," Pete said, and turned back to his beloved stove.

Jack did not like Whiley; he was afraid of the wiry man. Jack's eyes kept closing, so he got up and reluctantly left for a shower and bed . . . and horse liniment. Punching his pillow up, he settled into the bunk. He could still hear the "scraping" of Whiley's knife in the chow hall.

Off again the next morning on Star this time. Although Star gave him a sense of security, he liked Kicker's feistiness. He trotted the horse along the fence on the narrow trail. He loved the sky and this part of the ride with the hazy hills and mountains in the distance. The path itself was more challenging. Jack had to stop and try to remember the way down into a ravine and back up the other side.

He remembered this particularly steep ravine. It was where Frank had shot at the snake. Jack carefully dismounted and started leading Star. He broke out in a cold sweat, not wanting to walk in the ravine and especially not wanting to meet a rattler. He stopped, took a deep breath, loosened the pistol in its holster and, with a gulp, continued.

When he passed the place where they had encountered the snake, Jack heaved a sigh of relief. Nevertheless, he continued scanning the path nervously. At the top, he remounted Star and continued along the fence path.

He stopped for lunch at the same place they had before. Jack was satisfied with the way he had acted in the "snake ravine," as he named it. Confident now that he could handle ridin' fence as well as any other hand, Jack smiled to himself. However, he still checked carefully before sliding off Star and having lunch. This time he checked for scorpions and spiders also.

In the afternoon he took a break and went to see the wild cat print in the sand behind the large rock. He saw not one, but several paw prints. *"The same wild cat?"* Jack wondered,

"Or was there more than one?" He looked around but saw nothing. Jack's hair stood up on the back of his neck. Somewhere among the rocks and boulders he thought he saw a movement. A wild cat ready to pounce? Or was it the ghost of Don Cuervo de Vaca? Suddenly, he had an urgent need to leave.

The rest of the trip went easily and Jack began to feel as if he might make a good cowboy after all. For the next several weeks he rode fence on Monday, Tuesday, Thursday and Friday. Wednesdays and Saturdays he helped out around the stables and barn, but ropin' calves, he thought, was the most fun. He was getting better at it now. On Saturday nights the family went to town to see a movie. Sundays they went to church and came home to Mrs. Rollin's fried chicken, mashed potatoes and gravy, corn on the cob, and apple or cherry pie for dessert. Jack was beginning to enjoy a friendship with Ann. They had fun together and he was able to share some of his feelings with her. She had stopped laughing at him, and he had stopped teasing her . . . well, almost.

"Do you think Ann is in love with Jack?" asked Rachael?

"Oh phooey," pronounced Austin. "That's just stupid. Jack could never like Ann!"

"But he gave her his jacket..."

"That's just being a gentleman. Doesn't mean anything."

"Why don't we just continue the story and find

out?" Grandpa said and reached for a marshmallow.

"I hope this story doesn't become mushy," Austin mumbled.

Although Jack was becoming more accustomed to riding, he still was sore at the end of a long day. He also was very wary about rattlesnakes and wildcats, and jumped at any sound he heard while on the fence trail. Sometimes he would see a movement out of the corner of his eye, but when he turned to look, there was nothing there. This scared Jack, but he did not tell anyone about his fear because he knew he would be teased. From time to time he would stop and shoot at a cactus or a rock. He knew one day he would meet with a rattler and he wanted to be prepared for anything: wildcats, rattlesnakes or . . . who knows what else? *How do you shoot a ghost?'* he wondered.

CHAPTER FOURTEEN: The Ravine

Jack rode Star out of the back bunk house corral one morning in late July. At six in the morning it was already eighty degrees and he was not looking forward to the hot afternoon. He would have to take it easy and pace himself and Star.

An hour down the trail Jack found a broken strand of wire. He repaired it, noted the post number and continued down the path. As he rounded a curve near a ravine, the horse stopped suddenly. In the path a large rattle snake was coiled. Jack could hear the whirring rattle warning them off. Nervously pulling his pistol from its holster, he aimed and pulled the trigger. "Click" was its only response. Star, also frightened, tried to back up and Jack panicked. Scared out of his wits and yelling in fear, he changed the chambers of his pistol and shot again. This time he missed not just the snake, but the path also. Star, not able to back up anymore, reared up on her hind legs and sent Jack head over heels into the ravine below. The pistol flew from his hand and disappeared out of sight.

Swimming up to consciousness, Jack felt a pain in his arm. He opened his eyes but everything was fuzzy. He remembered that something dangerous was nearby, but could not remember just what it was. Jack drifted off into darkness again. Sometime later he woke up again and remembered the snake. Frightened, he tried to get up quickly and almost passed out when pain shot up his arm.

After a few minutes, Jack stood up slowly and looked for the snake. He noticed he was in a deep ravine. Looking up at the trail, Jack did not see Star anywhere. He started to sit on a rock but jumped up when he felt a stinging on his left leg. Had a scorpion stung him? No, he sighed in relief, looking down to find cactus thorns sticking out of his leg. He began to pull them out. If he had not been wearing chaps it might have been worse. *"Rolled over a cactus,"* he thought. *"Good grief, what next!"*

How was he going to explain this? Missed shooting a snake, lost his six-shooter, thrown by his horse, rolled over a cactus, and landed in a ravine with a hurt . . . broken? . . . arm. After removing as many spines as he could, Jack gently sat on the rock. His head was still spinning and he had difficulty concentrating. He bent over and placed his head between his legs. Soon the spinning stopped and his mind began to clear.

Dejected, in pain and disgusted, Jack sat staring at the ground. Something was wrong here. He could not make sense of what he saw. There were hoof marks in the dried mud. What was different about this? What did this mean? The dizziness and fuzziness of his brain made it hard to think. He closed his eyes, but his head started spinning even more. Then the thought broke out of the prison of his stunned mind.

"Rustlers! This must be the path the rustlers take."

Jack's excitement overcame his pain and discomfort. "I've got to see where these prints lead," he thought. He stood and, with unstable legs, followed the path. After fifteen minutes he came to the end of the canyon and the end of the tracks. They stopped at a large bolder set into the canyon wall. Pushing on the rock with all his strength, it didn't budge. Jack scratched his head with his good arm.

"I'd better go and report this," he said aloud, although there were no ears to hear him. Or were there? He looked around again, nervously, but saw no one. Jack knew he must try to get to the ranch house before it got dark. He looked at his watch and saw it was broken. He could not tell how long he had been out.

"Why didn't he just call the ranch on his cell phone?" Austin asked.

"In those days, Austin, there were no cell phones, no TV and certainly no electronic games," Grandpa

said.

"Wow! How did they survive without cell phones and digital games?"

"It was fairly simple. We called people on telephones and talked to our friends and neighbors face to face."

"Wow!" Austin said again. "I'm glad I did not live then. It must have been really boring."

Jack walked back to where he had fallen and started climbing up the side of the ravine. There in the dirt was his pistol. At least he had that back. Climbing the ravine was hard going with only one hand. Once he slid backward, but caught himself. The pain in his arm increased as Jack continued his ascent to the trail. On reaching it, he made a sling out of his bandanna and hung it around his neck. He could move his fingers painfully, so maybe his arm had not been broken. Jack checked the trail for the snake, but it was gone. Walking around the curve, the way he had come, he saw Star standing patiently on the trail, nibbling on some weeds.

"Sorry to leave you like that," Jack said apologetically as he tried to mount the horse. It was impossible to lift himself up. Finally, he led Star to a large boulder and used that, gritting his teeth with the pain in his arm. "We'd better get going."

Star did not want to go around the curve again and Jack had to urge her with gentle kicks with the spurs. It was very late so he went as fast as he could get Star to go. As he rode he thought about the rustlers. Was Whiley one of them? He sure looked mean and that knife of his was menacing. He could not help thinking that perhaps Jed was working with Whiley. After all, what did anyone know about Jed? And was Begay part of the gang? He kicked Star to make her go faster. *"One thing is certain,"* he thought. *"Ghosts don't herd cattle!"*

Just after sundown, he made his way through the looming darkness to the corral. Jimmy ran out of the stable.

"We were getting worried about you," he said. "'Bout ready to send out a posse." He looked at Jack's arm, "You all right? What happened?"

"Oh, I just fell," Jack said, deciding to save his information for Mr. Rollin. He wished Frank was still here, but he had left for ROTC camp and would not be back until August. Jimmy took his horse and Jack, too tired to care, limped to the house. Before he got there, Mrs. Rollin ran out with Ann trailing her.

"What happened? We were awfully worried about you," Mrs. Rollin said in a rush. "Oh, what happened to your arm? Come with me," she commanded, not waiting for Jack to answer.

Ann said nothing, but stood with worry reflected in her face.

Inside the house, Mrs. Rollin looked at his arm and declared a sprained wrist. She wrapped it up and sent him to wash and dress for dinner. "We've been waiting dinner for you." She said gruffly. Her toughness covered up her obvious concern for Jack.

"I can't yet," Jack said. "I have to talk to Mr. Rollin right now."

"Can't it wait for after dinner?" she asked.

"I think I'd better see him now. I have something important to tell him," Jack insisted.

Jack sat in a leather chair across the desk from Mr. Rollin. He told him about falling off his horse and falling into the ravine which led to a canyon. He told him of the cattle prints leading to a rock.

"You have had a rough time of it," Mr. Rollin said, shuffling some papers on his desk. "You must have hit your head very hard. I know of no such canyon."

"But it's true, Mr. Rollin," Jack said, frustrated.

"Well, we'll look into it."

"But..."

"Meanwhile Jack, don't talk to anyone about what you thought you saw. Now wash-up and we'll all be able to eat dinner."

Jack did as he was told, but wondered how he was going to convince Mr. Rollin that he actually saw the cattle prints in the canyon. How could Mr. Rollin not know about the canyon on his own land? He had to find out.

"It's always the same," Austin said.

"What?" asked Grandpa, happy for a break from the story.

"Grown-ups. They never believe us kids. Here Jack had some important information, but did Mr. Rollin believe him?" Austin threw up his arms, "Of course not!"

"You're correct. Sometimes adults don't listen when they should."

"What are we supposed to do?" asked Rachael. "Especially when it is important."

"I think the best thing to do is to indicate that what you are saying is very important. Yes, stress that you want to tell them something very important. That's about all you can do. Now, let's get back to the story."

CHAPTER FIFTEEN: Plans

After dinner Ann and Jack went into the patio. She questioned him about what had happened on the trail.

"Well," Jack said, rubbing his sore wrist as he told her of the snake and falling into the ravine, "I screwed it all up. I forgot to change to the loaded chamber of the pistol. Then I added to Star's fear when I yelled, which made her throw me."

"I'm just happy you didn't break your arm," Ann consoled, scooting closer to him on the bench.

"Mr. Rollin believes I hit my head too hard and wouldn't believe me." Jack wished he had not said this and hoped that Ann had not noticed.

"He wouldn't believe you?" Ann inquired. "He wouldn't believe what?"

Here it is, Jack thought. He would never convince Mr. Rollin, yet he needed someone to confide in. Frank, who would have been the best person, wasn't here, so he decided to tell Ann.

"Do you promise not to tell anyone what I'm about to tell you? I don't want any more people thinking I'm out of my mind." After Ann promised on a crossed heart, Jack described the cattle tracks in the mud of the canyon floor, and the boulder to which they led. When he finished they sat in silence for a few minutes.

"And my grandfather didn't believe you?" Ann looked at him and when her eyes met with Jack's he had to look away. He felt as if he could swim in the depths of those liquid green eyes.

"Mr. Rollin said he didn't know of any such canyon." Jack moved over on the bench, feeling uncomfortable being so near Ann.

She brushed back her unruly lock of hair and said, "I don't understand. Grandpa knows every inch of this ranch. How can he say he doesn't know about the ravine? He must have a reason for what he said. I just don't know what it could be." After a pause, she continued with enthusiasm, "That just leaves us one thing to do. We need to go out there and see if we can move the boulder and see what's behind it."

"I don't think that's such a good idea . . . for you to go, that is." Jack said. "It's too dangerous and you might get hurt."

"I'm as strong as you are, Tenderfoot!" Ann insisted. "I can take care of myself!"

Jack was saddened by her retreat to the way she had been when they first met. They sat in silence, staring into the night.

"Oh Jack, I'm sorry." Ann hung her head. "I'm just worried about you and I don't understand what Grandfather is trying to do."

"What I think we need to do is make a plan," Jack said, feeling better about Ann now.

"I agree."

"How about this?" Jack asked. "My next trip through there, I'll go down into the canyon and check all around for more clues."

"I'll come too!" Ann exclaimed.

"Please Ann, you stay home," Jack pleaded. "I know you can take care of yourself and maybe later you can come with me. I don't want to attract attention to our find just yet. This time let me make a reconnaissance to see how the land lays," he continued, hoping he had not made her angry again.

"You sound like a movie sound track," she laughed. "All right, this time I'll stay home. But you can bet I'll go with you when you get back again. We have to figure this out. I wish Frank was here. He'd know what to do."

"I wish he was here too, but he's not. That means we'll have to do what we can. We can't trust anyone, including your grandfather."

That Saturday Jack and Ann were relegated to cleaning out the barn. Ann had to do the shoveling of the cow manure while Jack, because of his sprained wrist, hosed the cement floors down. As they worked they talked in low voices about Mr. Rollin's reaction, but they could not understand what he was hiding. He couldn't be stealing his own cattle. Finally, they gave up the discussion and talked about going into town that evening.

After dinner, the family got into the Ford station wagon and, as usual, drove the twenty miles into Bluff. By this time, Jack and Ann had developed a set itinerary. First, they would visit Bluff Notions to see if they had anything of interest this week. Jack always bought a carton of Cinnamon Chiclets gum. Most of the cowhands either smoked or chewed tobacco. He chewed gum. It helped when he was on the trail to keep his mouth from drying out. Ann always looked wistfully at the jewelry. There was a silver pendant she wanted, but did not want to spend the money. It was round and had a design of a horse engraved into it. After the hardware store they went to the movies, which started at 7:30. This particular night they were showing "Rio Grande" with John Wayne.

"I wish we could figure out who the bad guys are as fast as John Wayne did," Ann said as she scooped the cherry off the top of her sundae. She and Jack went to the drug store soda fountain as usual after the movie. Ann always had a strawberry sundae while Jack stuck with hot fudge.

"Yeah," Jack agreed, licking some fudge off his upper lip with his tongue. "On my way back on Tuesday I'll go down again into the ravine and see if I can find out anything else."

"Let me go with you. I can find a way to sneak out and meet you on the trail." Ann pleaded.

"No way!" Jack stated more emphatically than he had intended. He saw Ann's neck begin to turn red, a sure sign she was getting angry. "What I mean Ann," Jack began to placate her, "is that we can't make a move until we get more information ... evidence. And it might be dangerous." He concluded, "I wouldn't want you to get hurt."

"I can take care of myself," she stated, but her anger seemed to abate somewhat.

"I know you can, but I'd like to have someone at the ranch know where I am. Just in case something should happen to me," Jack rationalized. He wasn't sure he wanted to go down into the canyon alone, but he knew something had to be done.

Jack did not sleep well Sunday night. Tossing and turning in his sleep, he dreamed of Whiley cornering him and threatening to slit his throat with that very sharp knife. In another dream Begay, dressed as an Indian, tied him to a post and danced around him before lighting the logs stacked under his feet. When he awoke he was wet with sweat.

In the semi-darkness he dressed and went to breakfast. Everyone seemed to be full of cheer and expecting a great day except for Ann, who looked very worried, and himself.

Jimmy came over as he saddled Kicker.

"You look like your best friend just kicked the bucket," Jimmy said, laying his hand on Jack's shoulder. "What's wrong?"

"Nothing," Jack said. Just didn't sleep well last night."

"Well, you take care. Don't fall asleep on Star," he chuckled.

CHAPTER SIXTEEN: Kidnapped

Jack rode wearily along the trail. The question kept coming back to him: Why was Mr. Rollin acting like he did not know about the ravine? After all it was his ranch, he had grown up here. Why would Mr. Rollin refuse to believe him? Jack didn't have the answers, but he knew he would have a large piece of the puzzle when he did.

Arriving at the bunkhouse at twilight, Jack groomed and fed Star and went in to eat. He was happy that Pete did not mother him as much now and the rest of the men seemed to accept him. After dinner, Jed asked him if he wanted to join in the ever present poker game.

"I'm not very good at poker," Jack said, trying to decide if he wanted to play poker with these guys. Sometimes the games seemed to get loud and rough.

"Oh, come on," the slightly overweight man insisted. "We just play for pennies."

"Well, all right." Jack pulled out a chair and sat. Whiley, Tork, Begay, and Matt were the other players around the table.

The men were drinking beer as they played, and the conversation covered a whole realm of things. At first Jack did not listen; as he was too busy concentrating on his hands, but soon he relaxed and felt more at ease. He won a few hands but bailed out of bad hands before he had invested too much money in bets.

"Tell us why you keep that scarf around your neck, Matt," Whiley asked, grinning.

"None of your business," Matt replied softly. Jack had heard rumors that Matt had a terrible scar on his neck from some kind of fight up north.

"Now Matt, we're your friends." Whiley continued, his lips curled in a sneer.

"You gonna bet or talk, Whiley?" Tork demanded.

"Gonna do both," Whiley replied. "Raise ya five." He shoved some chips into the center of the table. Then he turned to Matt. "Well, you gonna show us your neck?"

"Leave him alone," Tork said, throwing in his hand. "I'm out."

Jack looked at his hand, four aces. "Raise you five."

"You must have a hot hand," Jed said. "I think you're bluffing. I'll see your five and call."

Jack laid down his hand and Jed sighed.

"You're a pretty good poker player for a youngen'."

"Had a good teacher," Jack replied, handing his cards to Matt who was dealer for the next hand. Jack had to admit he also was curious about Matt's neck scarf. He would sure like to hear that story.

"Hey, Begay," Whiley said. "You know what's under Matt's scarf?"

"His neck," Begay grunted, taking a long drink from his bottle of beer. Jack could see that Begay did not want any part of this discussion.

"Let's play poker," Tork said with authority. He was the back foreman, after all.

"Say, Tork," Jed said. "I need to go to the main house tomorrow. Mr. Rollin asked me to help Jimmy break a new horse."

"No problem. Just get back here as soon as you can." Tork looked at his cards.

Jack did not know of any horses that needed breaking. But then he did not know all the workings of the ranch. He yawned and threw his hand in.

"I'm out," he said, collecting his money. "I've got to get some sleep."

As he lay in bed, he thought again about Mr. Rollin's reluctance to believe in him. He thought also of Whiley and his knife. He sure seemed to be a mean, and maybe dangerous, person. He yawned again and smiled. At least he had won two dollars and seventeen cents.

Jack rode out at first light, after having Pete stuff him with eggs, bacon, hash browns and milk. He liked Pete and found it hard to refuse the food. He was thankful it was a little cooler this morning. He pulled his jacket around his neck and nudged Kicker into a fast trot. He had to make up time if he was to investigate the ravine today. He skipped stopping for lunch. He would eat in the ravine while he looked for clues.

Tying Kicker to a dead piece of shrub, he half climbed and half slid down the side of the ravine into the canyon floor. This time he missed sliding over any cactus. At the bottom, he sat on a rock, ate one of his sandwiches, and took a gulp of water from his canteen. As he chewed, he looked around the canyon floor and would have gasped if his mouth had not been full of a baloney sandwich. There were no tracks. He dropped his sandwich and walked toward the boulder where the prints had ended before.

"Nothing," he thought. *"No prints. Did the fall I took give me hallucinations? Maybe there really was a ghost."* Jack, beginning to doubt himself, went back to his seat, picked up his sandwich, brushed it off and took a gritty bite. *"No, there were tracks . . . a lot of them. And they led to that boulder,"* he thought. *"I'm not crazy. I did see them and they were real."* He finished his sandwich and looked around the canyon more carefully. Then he noticed that there were brush marks across the trail. Someone had attempted to hide the evidence of the tracks.

He looked around and felt as if someone was watching

him. He went to the boulder and tried to move it but could not budge it. He examined it carefully and saw part of the print of a horse shoe. This was the place! There had been at least one horseman here who had tried to clean up the evidence. But who?

Jack scrambled up the ravine, in a hurry to get back to the ranch and tell Ann what he had found. All the way back he thought about Mr. Rollin's refusal to believe him. Who had brushed the tracks away? Whiley . . . Begay . . . Mr. Rollin? How was he going to find the answers? What would Frank do?

When he arrived at the ranch, there was much confusion. He unsaddled his horse and stabled him, wondering why Jimmy had not met him as usual. He noticed that several horses were gone. He hurried to feed and brush Kicker and ran to the ranch house.

Entering the door, he saw Mrs. Rollin sitting in a chair weeping with her face in her hands. Next to her Mr. Rollin stood with a scowl. His face was red with anger and concern.

"What's happening?" Jack asked, looking from one to the other.

"Ann's disappeared," Mr. Rollin said. "Do you know where she could have gone?" he demanded.

"No sir," Jack said, but had some reservations about his statement. "When was she last seen?"

"This morning," Mrs. Rollin, eyes red from crying and face lined with worry, said as she wiped her eyes. "She said she was going for a ride. But..."

"She's not been seen since," Mr. Rollin continued for his wife, who had begun to weep again. "I've had everyone out looking for her since four this afternoon."

Jack calculated that was a little more than two hours ago. They should have found her by now. "Maybe . . ." Jack started to say.

"Maybe what?" Mr. Rollin interrupted sternly.

"Maybe she went looking for the rustlers. I . . . uh . . . told her about the prints I saw in the canyon."

"You told her? I told you to tell no one!" Mr. Rollin shouted in rage. "Now you have put my granddaughter in danger and ruined my plans to capture the rustlers."

"I stopped by there a few hours ago and there was no sign of her."

"You saw nothing?" Mrs. Rollin said, wiping tears from her face with her apron.

"No Ma'am. But someone had brushed away the hoof prints."

"Why in God's name did you tell Ann? I told you to tell no one," Mr. Rollin said, worry and anxiety shadowing his face.

"I'm sorry. I thought you didn't believe me and I . . ." Jack, who felt tears filling his eyes, could not continue for fear of crying. He turned on his heel and ran out the door to the stables. He heard Mr. Rollin calling after him but paid no attention. He re-saddled Kicker and headed up the trail toward the canyon.

"Jack, come back! it's dangerous up there!" Mr. Rollin yelled, but Jack did not hear him. He was only thinking about Ann being in the hands of the rustlers. What would they do to her? She must have stumbled on them as they were cleaning up the tracks. He urged Kicker on faster.

"I'm scared, Grandpa," Rachael said, her eyes wide. "I don't want Ann to get hurt." She scooted over toward his chair and took his hand in hers.

Grandpa felt Rachael's hand gripping his so hard that he felt it might come off his arm if she squeezed any harder. He wondered if he should continue with the story.

"Aw Rachael. Jack told her not to go near the canyon." Austin turned to his grandfather. "Besides, this is just a story. Tell her, Grandpa, it's just a story."

"I don't know if I should continue this story. If you have nightmares about this, your grandma will kill me. I think I'll stop for the night."

"You can't!" Austin exclaimed. "You can't leave the story like this!"

"It's OK, Grandpa," Rachael said, loosening up on her grip. "I won't be afraid. I promise."

"I think I'll have to think it over tonight, see if I think I should finish it or not." He thought a moment, scratching his head. Then he pushed himself up from the easy chair.

"Please, Grandpa," both kids said in unison, not wanting to quit for the night.

"Let's clean up and go to bed. I'll see if I will continue the story tomorrow."

CHAPTER SEVENTEEN: The Outlaw

Urging Kicker on as fast as he could, Jack followed the trail he had just come down. He knew he had to hurry. There were only a few hours of daylight left. When he could he galloped, but most of the time he went at a fast trot. Would he ever get to the ravine? Would he recognize the place where he was thrown? He nudged Kicker with his spurs to keep him moving fast.

Jack slowed down to make a sharp bend in the trail around an outcrop. As he came around the turn, he pulled Kicker to a halt. On the trail, blocking the way with his horse, was Whiley.

"Where are you going so fast?" Whiley sneered, steadying his horse.

"Haven't you heard? Ann has disappeared."

"Yeah, I heard," Whiley said, adjusting the reins in his hand.

"We've got to find her quickly." Jack felt fear rising in his chest. What was Whiley going to do? He kept his eye on the knife in Whiley's belt.

"You know where she is, I suppose." Whiley reached into his shirt pocket, pulled out a bag of tobacco and started rolling a cigarette with one hand.

Jack was too scared to be impressed. He was worried about Ann, and now Whiley was making him waste time. Was he in league with the rustlers? He was afraid of Whiley's knife. What could he do? He had not even thought to pick up his gun before leaving the ranch house. Was Whiley going to try to stop him from reaching Ann?

"He's going to kill me!" Jack's mind screamed. It took all his courage not to turn and run, but Ann's life was at stake and he felt responsible for her.

"Get out of my way, Whiley," Jack commanded with as much conviction as he could muster. He could almost feel Whiley's knife thudding into his chest.

"If you are sure you know where she is, I'll go with you," Whiley said, pulling his horse back off the trail. "Go ahead. I'll follow you."

Jack, waiting for a knife in his back, went on up the trail as fast as he could. He did not know what else he could do. The hair on the nape of his neck stood up, waiting for Whiley to make his move. But nothing happened. Jack began to feel that perhaps Whiley was not one of the gang. But what if he was?

After another half hour, Jack found the spot where he

had been thrown. He dismounted.

"It's down here," he told Whiley, pointing to the ravine.

"How would you know?" Whiley smirked, not believing Jack.

Jack, exasperated now, said with anger, "I know because I was thrown here. I fell down that ravine and found cattle prints." The story spilled out of him like water from a broken dam.

"What are you standin' there for, boy?" Whiley asked, dismounting. "Let's get down there pronto."

The two scrambled down the side of the ravine and into the canyon. They attempted to move the great rock, but could not. Whiley looked around and spotted a good sized tree branch.

"Looks like they used this to move the boulder," Whiley said as he placed the end of the branch between the rock and the cliff face. Though both of them heaved on the pole, the boulder refused to move.

"It can't be done," Jack said with tears of frustration in his eyes.

"We have to be able to open this cave," Whiley said, hauling on the branch again.

"You're . . . right! They . . . opened . . . it," Jack said, grasping and pulling on the pole.

Again they heaved with all their strength, straining themselves to the breaking point. The boulder moved a few inches, a foot, and then opened all the way, exposing a deep cave.

They fell to the ground in exhaustion.

"It's too dark in there," Jack, looking into the cave, said. "We need flashlights. I've got one in my saddle bag."

"So do I," gasped Whiley, trying to catch his breath. "I just hope they work."

"I'll get them," Jack said. He scrambled up the ravine and retrieved the flashlights from their saddle bags. Then he slid back down the embankment, narrowly missing the cactus, and handed a flashlight to Whiley.

Whiley stood up. "I'll go in. You wait here in case help arrives. You can tell them what's happened." Whiley carefully entered the cave. Soon Jack could see neither Whiley nor his light.

Jack paced back and forth in front of the cave mouth, stopping every so often to listen. But he heard nothing from within the cave or from the trail. It was getting dark, and Jack felt he had been waiting there hours. Had something happened to Whiley? That he might be one of the rustlers kept rising into Jack's consciousness. No, he put that thought out of his mind. Didn't Whiley have trouble opening the cave? One of the gang would know an easier way to move the rock. No, Jack thought, Whiley was not one of them. If he was not, then where was he? Was he in trouble? And where was Ann?

CHAPTER EIGHTEEN: The Cave

"What happened to Ann?" Rachael asked. "Where did she go?"

"Well now," grandpa said, as he shifted in his seat to get more comfortable. "We've got to go back in time to when Jack left on his fence ride."

The day after Jack left for his round of the fence line, Ann wandered around aimlessly. She had been this way since Jack left. This morning her grandmother had asked her to feed the chickens. She filled a bucket with chicken feed and wandered over to the chicken pen. As she spread the grain on the ground the chickens gathered around her, clucking loudly.

A vision of their contest to rope hens came into her mind. She gave out a little laugh which strangely turned to tears.

The tears turned into a sob.

"Darn that Jack," she said to the chickens. "Darn him!"

"Why did he go by himself? I could have gone. Does he think I'm a weakling?"

She threw some more grain on the ground and stood looking at the birds.

What was happening? Were there rustlers? Probably. But what part did her grandfather have to do with the whole thing? After her father, she loved her grandfather best, but it seemed as if he was betraying her.

Ann went over to the pail rack and hung up the basket. Then she stood staring at the pail, trying to make up her mind. She nodded, turned and hurried to the stables. There she saddled her horse Sally. As she was about to mount, Ann remembered she would need some supplies. She tied the horse to the back porch railing and quietly entered the kitchen.

"Can help you?" Chin asked with his usual smile.

"I'm going to go for a ride and thought I might take some food with me . . . in case I . . .er . . . get hungry."

"Sure, missy." Chin dashed into the pantry and after a few minutes came out with a bag. "Don't forget water," he reminded her. "Where you go?"

"I don't know." Ann took the bag and looked in. It contained a sandwich and an apple. "I just thought I'd ride out and think."

"Be careful, Miss Ann. There are snakes," Chin warned.

Ann smiled and thanked Chin. Grabbing a canteen, she

filled it and was soon off, but not to "ride out and think." She knew exactly where she was going. To find the cave Jack had found.

Two hours later she reached the area of the ranch that was filled with canyons and ravines. She had to slow down and find her way around and through them.

She noticed a small cloud of dust. Someone was moving cattle over the next ridge and she decided to investigate. As she got near, Ann saw four men herding about twenty head of cattle. She recognized one of them as one of the ranch's cowboys. It was that nasty skinny Jed who had made fun of them when they started roping calves.

Determined to find out where they were going, she followed, attempting to keep a good distance between herself and the herd. Hiding behind several boulders, Ann saw them enter a gorge which must have been near the fence line of the ranch. A cowboy blocked the exit from the ravine to keep the cattle in and the other three men disappeared around a bend in the canyon wall.

She waited awhile, but nothing seemed to happen. Hungry, she opened her sandwich and took a bite. Just as she swallowed, she found herself in the grip of a very strong man. She spit out the half-chewed bit of sandwich and screamed as loud as she could, kicking all the while.

Then another hand covered her mouth so hard she could hardly breath. Too surprised to be frightened, she hit out with her fist.

"Hold on their, girlie!" A man's voice commanded. "It

ain't goin' to do you no good."

Ann kicked out even harder and tried to pull the man's hand off her mouth.

"Now girlie, you gonna hurt yourself if you keep this up."

The man dragged her down from her perch and into the canyon. By now she had no more strength.

"Go find her horse and bring it in," called the man who held her. "Be sure you sweep the area clean before closing up."

It was almost dark now. Jack worried that he had neither seen nor heard from Whiley. He made the decision to go in and find out what was happening for himself. He checked the flashlight, gathered up his courage, and entered the evil darkness of the cave.

The cave was wide and tall enough for Jack to walk in. It twisted and turned until he felt as if he was going in circles. Several times he came to tunnels going off the main cave. He decided to keep to the largest passage. After all, they had herded cattle through here. If he had not already known that, he would have guessed it from the smell and the cow patties he stepped in from time to time.

Jack moved along with his back to the cave wall. He heard voices up ahead and slowed down, trying to hear what was being said.

"Boss . . . don't . . .she . . ." one voice said.

"I don't . . . what she . . . ," boomed a much deeper voice.

As he listened, he noticed his flashlight was growing dim.

He turned it off to save the batteries and crept nearer the sound of the voices.

A hand closed over his mouth.

Jack tried to yell.

He kicked out, but found nothing but air. Twisting and trying to hit the person holding him, he found a finger in his mouth and bit down hard.

"Ouch!" yelled a familiar voice and the hand was jerked away from his mouth. He started to yell, but the hand was replaced. "Give me some help!" demanded the man. "This kid's stronger than he looks." The voice was someone he definitely knew but in his struggling he could not identify him. *Must be Whiley.* He was one of them after all. He had waited for Jack to come in so he could catch him.

Now a second pair of hands gripped him.

"We have him now," said an excited man, whose voice was unfamiliar to him. "Might as well give up struggling, kid."

It was over and Jack stopped fighting. The hands holding him were too strong.

Something was stuffed into his mouth. His arms were pulled behind his back and his hands were tied. Then he was pushed along the cave and through a narrow passage. He was half shoved, half thrown into a room, landing on the hard stone floor. His eyes blinked rapidly in the light of a kerosene lantern which lit the room.

Looking up, Jack saw a man sitting on a crate. He was in his 50's, pudgy around the middle, with a mean crinkling face and piggy eyes set close together and so small you could hardly see them. To his right stood a strange cowpoke, who was leaning against the cave wall chewing on a wad of tobacco. He spat a stream of tobacco juice which narrowly missed Jack's face.

"Take the gag out of his mouth," the pudgy man said. "No one can hear him here."

"OK Boss," said the voice from behind him. Jack knew that voice, and was now sure that it was not Whiley's. A hand untied the gag and, as the cloth came out of Jack's mouth, he saw Jed.

"You!" Jack exclaimed.

"Yeah, me," said Jed with a grin.

Jack noticed he had a blood stained handkerchief wrapped around his hand. The result of my bite, Jack thought.

"Who's with you?" asked the "Boss."

"No one," Jack lied, thinking that if they did not know about Whiley he certainly wasn't going to tell them.

"You couldn't open the cave by yourself," sneered the tobacco chewing rustler.

"I did anyway," Jack said.

Jed picked Jack up by the hair.

"Ouch!" he cried, thinking he was going to lose all his hair. Tears of pain and anger formed in his eyes and ran down his cheeks.

"Who's with you?" Jed asked the question again.

"No . . . one," Jack repeated, wanting to scream with the

pain.

"Put him down, Jed," the boss commanded. "He'll tell us soon enough."

"I opened it myself," Jack bellowed in anger when Jed released him. "I used a pole I found outside."

"You little punk," said the Boss. "You almost ruined my plans for the Rollin R ranch. I was succeeding in increasing my herd while decreasing the Rolling R's herd." He laughed a crazy kind of laugh and then was quiet for a moment. The flickering lantern light gave his face a diabolical look.

He put his head back, laughed again and said, "Well, I've done pretty well so far. Perhaps they'll never find this cave."

"What do you want us to do with the boy?" Jed asked.

"Throw him in the other room. If there is anyone with him, we have hostages," said the Boss. "Then search the cave," he added.

CHAPTER NINETEEN: We're Gonna Die!

J ack was picked up by his shirt collar and shoved down another tunnel and into a smaller cave. They dumped him on the dirt floor. The small room was lit only by a single lantern.

"Have fun with your girlfriend," the tobacco spitting man said, shooting a spray of tobacco juice in toward a dark corner where Ann was hunched down. Then he and Jed left.

Ann sat there, dazed.

"Ann," Jack said across the six feet that separated them. "Ann, are you all right?"

"Is . . . that . . . really you . . . Jack?" she asked softly, her voice shaky.

"Yes, I'm here. Are you hurt?"

"No . . . not much. I have a few bruises and these ropes are cutting off the circulation to my hands." Her voice was stronger now.

Jack rolled over close to Ann. Twisting and shoving with his feet, he got himself into a sitting position.

"I couldn't believe it was you," Ann said. "I thought I was dreaming."

"It really is me, but I'm not going to be much help tied up like this."

"I'm so scared," Ann said, her voice still shaky.

"Don't worry. We'll get out of this somehow. Your father has the whole ranch looking for you." He wondered what had happened to Whiley, but he didn't want to say anything in case Jed was listening. "How did you get here?"

"I was a stupnagle . . ." she stifled a sob.

Jack gave her time to compose herself.

"I was stupid," Ann repeated. She seemed to be able to talk now. "I was mad at you for telling me to stay home. So I saddled Sally and came looking for the canyon." She slowly told him how she had been caught and brought here.

"There must be a way to escape," Jack said, struggling with the ropes that tied his hands. All he succeeded in doing was tightening them.

"I haven't been able to loosen my ropes either," Ann sighed. She was quiet a minute. "Jack?"

"Yes."

"I'm sorry I didn't listen to you." She started weeping

quietly.

"Don't worry Ann. We'll get out of this. Just give me time to think."

Jack surveyed the chamber. It was oval in shape, with a sloping ceiling. Across from them was the opening leading back to where the Boss and his henchmen had been. Near the door was a small cask or barrel. Jack looked closer. Printed on the barrel was "DANGER: BLACK POWDER." It was blasting powder. On the other side of the opening a kerosene lamp was burning on the floor. At least they did not put the lamp on the blasting powder, he thought. There was nothing else in the room but Ann and him. Not even a sharp stone he could use to cut their bonds. Jack, now exhausted, leaned his head back against the wall. He looked up and couldn't believe his eyes. There was a smallish opening just above him.

"Ann, look above you."

She looked and saw the hole in the cave ceiling.

"If we can stand up maybe we can get out through the hole," Jack said hopefully.

"It's awfully high up."

Jack tried to stand but the ropes that tied his hands and feet were too tight. Ann tried with the same results. They fell back against the wall.

"There must be some way." Jack, frustrated, struggled in vain against the rope.

"There . . . is no . . . way," Ann said. "We can't . . ." Her voice gave out with a long sigh.

They lay there for a long time. Jack tried to think of a way out, but he could not devise a plan. Then he heard voices in the other room.

"There's no one here . . ."

"Must have . . . by himself."

"What will . . . do . . . ?"

"I told you to cover. . . tracks."

"I did, Boss . . ."

"We'll have to kill them. Make . . . like . . . an accident."

Jack felt sweat break out on his forehead. *"They're gonna kill us!"* He renewed his struggles to get out of the bonds, but all he was able to do was tighten the ropes which cut deeper into his wrists. He lay back and stared at the hole in the wall above him. *If only . . .*

Jack jumped as a head appeared in the hole. It was Whiley. He put his hand to his lips, indicating they should be quiet. He tried to get in through the hole, but he was too big. He withdrew his head. Then Jack saw Whiley's hand with his knife in it.

Swish . . . thunk! The knife stuck in the dirt about an inch from Jack's arm. At first Jack thought Whiley was trying to kill him, but remembering his aim with a knife, he knew Whiley would not have missed if that had been his goal.

He wiggled over and, turning his back, tried to saw the rope on his wrists. But he was afraid. *"What if I cut my wrists? I'll bleed to death!"*

"Come on, Jack. Hurry!" Whiley whispered.

"I know you can do it," joined Ann.

He screwed up his courage and tried again, pushing harder against the razor sharp knife. Jack came near to stabbing himself in the back, but with a sudden relief of pressure, he felt the rope part. Jack was now very thankful that Whiley kept the blade extremely sharp. He sat up and quickly cut the rope on his feet. When he stood up, the pins and needles in his legs and feet gave him so much pain that he winced and gave a little yelp.

"Shush," Whiley whispered. "Get the girl up here."

"Hurry, oh hurry, Jack," Ann said in her excitement.

"Hush, Ann, they'll hear us," Jack whispered, cutting the rope off her wrists and legs.

"I don't know if I can stand," Ann said. "My feet are asleep."

"I'll help," Jack picked her up, ignoring the pins and needles in his own legs and feet.

"Oooh, it hurts," Ann moaned.

"Come on, Ann," he said as he lifted her up to the hole. Whiley reached out and pulled her through. Jack jumped up, caught the edge of the hole, and tried to pull himself through when he heard the sound of running feet.

"They're getting away!" cried the Boss. "Stop them!"

Jack had his head and shoulders through the hole and thought he was going to escape but Jed caught his ankle.

"Got you now, you scroungie little brat!" Jed grabbed

Jack's other foot.

He felt himself being pulled back down out of the hole.

"Whiley! Help!" Jack hollered. Whiley grabbed his shoulders and pulled. Jack felt like the rope in a tug of war. His legs felt disjointed and he knew he was going to be pulled apart. If Jed got him he would be a dead cowboy. He could hardly stand the pain anymore.

"Hey! That's not fair. Jack is not supposed to die," Austin objected.

"Have patience," replied Grandpa, "let's see what happens."

Suddenly his legs were released and he heard loud voices in the cave behind him.

"Put your hands up!" It sounded like Mr. Rollin. "You heard me, Jed. If you reach for that pistol, you're dead." There was the sound of a pistol hitting the floor. "Well, if it isn't Bill Jenkins, my honorable neighbor. I'm not surprised to see you here."

"Down on your stomachs," said Begay. Jack could tell that voice anywhere.

"Come out of that hole now, Jack" said Mr. Rollin. "And where's Ann?"

"She's all right, Mr. Rollin," Jack said. "Boy am I glad to see you! They were going to kill us. If it hadn't been for Whiley . . ."

"Hi, Grandpa," cried Ann from the hole overhead. "I'll be right down. Whiley knows an easier way." A few minutes later Ann, followed by Whiley, entered the room. Ann ran to her grandfather and hugged him, then turned to Jack and did the same.

"Thank you, Jack. You saved me." Jack's face reddened.

"Thank Whiley. He's the one who saved us." Jack turned to Whiley. "I need to ask for your forgiveness, Whiley."

"Why's that?"

"Because I thought you were one of them. How can I ever thank you? I was worried about you. Where were you?"

"Oh, I went into the cave far enough to hear these bozzos talking, and came back using these round-about tunnels. Thought they might be useful when we came back."

"We?" asked Jack.

"Yeah, when I got back out of the cave I couldn't find you anywhere. I skedaddled, headed toward the ranch for help, and that's when I met Mr. Rollin and Begay."

"We must have passed each other. When I was going into the main tunnel, you were going out through a side tunnel."

"Let's get out of here," said Mr. Rollin. "Begay and Whiley, you take these skunks out. We'll hand them over to the sheriff. It's too bad we don't hang cattle rustlers anymore. I'm tempted."

"My pleasure," Whiley said, grabbing Jed and the other rustler roughly by their shirt collars. Begay seized the Boss, and dragged him after Whiley.

"Mr. Rollin," Jack said.

"Yes, Jack?"

"If you want to seal the cave, there's a barrel of blasting powder there." He pointed to the keg by the wall.

Mr. Rollin looked closely at the barrel. "Maybe we ought to leave now. I'll get Buddy to make good use of this blasting powder. But let's go. That stuff makes me uncomfortable."

Fifteen minutes later they were all outside talking. Ann had caught hold of Jack's hand and wouldn't let go. Jack turned red again.

By this time Buddy, the foreman, had arrived with a few other hands.

"Let's see where the tunnel ends," Mr. Rollin suggested. He and Buddy re-entered the cave. After about ten minutes they returned.

"Well," said Mr. Rollin, "I can hardly believe it. The cave empties into "Boss" Jenkins pasture. I've been watching him for two years now. His herds have increased too fast for it to be natural growth. He was pretty slick, but not slick enough."

"Is that why you told me to be quiet about the cave?" Jack asked. "I thought you didn't believe me."

"I believed you all right. I wanted to catch Jenkins red-handed." Mr. Rollin smiled. "I guess we did just that."

Mr. Rollin sent Buddy back to set the explosion and close the tunnel once and for all. Then he made everyone get out of the canyon. Soon Buddy came running out. There was a muffled explosion which shook the ground, and a cloud of smoke and dust was blown out of the cave entrance.

"That's that," concluded Mr. Rollin. "We better get you both back to the ranch house. Mrs. Rollin is probably going crazy with worry." He clapped Jack on the shoulder. "Nice going, Jack," he said with a smile.

"I knew Whiley was all right," said Austin, gloating.

"You were indeed correct," Grandpa said with a smile.

"And Jack saved Ann's life," sighed Rachael.

"Is that the end of the story?" asked Austin.

"No...no there's more. But that's enough for tonight. Time for bed everyone."

CHAPTER TWENTY: The Hero

There was great excitement when the group arrived back at the ranch house. Mrs. Rollin, crying, hugged Ann and then hugged Jack until he thought he would break. The hands gathered around to hear and rehear the story of the capture of the rustlers. Then the sheriff came and Jack had to retell the story for what seemed like the hundredth time.

Jenkins, Jed and the tobacco spitting rustler, who turned out to be a man named Jake who was wanted in Oklahoma for rustling, were handcuffed and placed in the back of the sheriff's car and taken to the county jail. Jack was bone tired and could hardly keep his eyes open. The adrenaline coursing through his blood had started to wear off.

"We must give these children something to eat and get them to bed," Mrs. Rollin insisted. "It's nearly one in the morning." Although Jack was not very hungry, he managed to eat a sandwich and gulp down a glass of milk. Next came a hot shower and bed. He was asleep before his head hit the pillow.

Jack woke up late the next morning in a cold sweat. He had dreamed that Jed was pulling his foot off and he could not escape. The sun was shining through the window and he could hear the birds singing. It was over, really over. Jack smiled to himself. Maybe he had gotten taller with all the pulling yesterday. He started to get up, but fell back into the bed. He felt like a bull had tossed him. The second time he tried he succeeded. He took another hot shower, which eased his pain. When he went into the dining room he felt famished, but knew it was too late for breakfast.

"You want eat?" Chin said with a wide grin. "You have anything you want. You hero."

"Thanks Chin, but I'm no hero. Can you get me a peanut butter and jam sandwich?"

"Everyone say you a hero. I get food. You sit."

Ann came into the dining room, looking as if she also had been run over. "If I look as bad as you look," she said, "I'm in a very bad way."

Jack laughed. "We both probably look bad, but we're alive and we have had a real adventure."

"How can you call it an adventure? We were kidnapped, tied up, put in a cave room, and almost killed."

"You're right there, but then that's what an adventure is. My father once told me that when you go through tough life threatening situations and survive to tell about it, that's an adventure."

"Using that definition, we really did have an adventure. Perhaps too much of an adventure." Ann made a face and brushed back her hair.

Jack laughed. "You're right. But the important part is we survived."

"You . . ."

Chin came in, interrupting Ann.

"Here food for Hero." He placed a plate of fried eggs, ham, hash browns and biscuits before both of them.

"All I asked for was a peanut butter sandwich," Jack reminded Chin.

"Oh, I got," Chin said with a smile as he placed a small plate with a peanut butter sandwich on it. "Heroes need lot of food."

"Chin's right, you know," Ann said after serving breakfast to Jack and herself.

"About having to eat lots of food?"

"No," Ann said patiently. "About you being a hero."

"I'm no such thing!" Jack said emphatically. He did not want to be a hero. He certainly did not feel like one.

"But you are," Ann said blushing. "You saved me and you exposed the rustlers. Grandfather was able to retrieve many of his lost cattle. You saved him thousands of dollars."

"I just stumbled, perhaps thrown would be a better word, into the situation."

"Yes, but you endangered your life for me." Ann reached her hand across the table to take Jack's. He quickly pulled it back and pretended to straighten his napkin. Ann's face reddened as she slowly took her hand back. They ate the rest of their breakfast in silence.

"There they are." Mrs. Rollin came into the room with a huge smile covering her face. "Finally up, I see. I can't tell you how happy I am to see you both alive and well."

"Shouldn't I be ridin' fence today?" Jack asked, looking for an excuse to get away and think things over.

"Not today. Today and tomorrow you both rest." Mrs. Rollin commanded. "Tomorrow night we are going to have a great celebration," she continued. "A bar-b-que and square dance in the old barn. The whole ranch and our neighbors—our good neighbors, that is—will be there."

Ann brightened up. "But I have nothing to wear to a party."

"We'll go to town today and buy you a party dress," said Mrs. Rollin, beaming.

After lunch, Ann and Mrs. Rollin went to town. But before they left, Jack took Mrs. Rollin aside and whispered something in her ear.

Jack, who wanted to get away from everybody, saddled Kicker and rode slowly out into the south pasture. He was no longer sore from riding, but he was bruised from the adventure. He thought how Ann had teased him and called

166

him a Tenderfoot when they had first met. She could not call him that anymore. He liked Ann, but was filled with confusion. At times he wanted to hold her hand, perhaps put his arm around her. Then other times he felt it was silly.

Turning his thoughts away from Ann, he thought about riding fence and being a cowboy. It was hard work, and now he found it could be very dangerous. He had almost been killed. But he had survived and felt very happy and proud of what he had done. Jack knew also that if he had stopped to think about what he was doing, he would have run away to hide. One thing he knew for sure. Being a real cowboy was not like being a movie cowboy.

Mr. Rollin called Jack into his office before dinner. "Jack," he said, "it was a foolish, yet brave, thing you did yesterday. Not only did you save Ann, but you saved me a lot of cattle."

Jack didn't know what to say.

"For this reason I'm giving you this check for your college fund."

Jack took the check and almost fell off his chair. It was made out for one thousand dollars.

"I can't take this," Jack said, embarrassed. "I was just doing what any hand would do in an emergency."

"You are one of my best hands," Mr. Rollin smiled. "But you earned this bonus. Take it and start a college fund, if you don't already have one."

"Yes, sir," Jack said. "And thank you for everything."

"You're welcome. Now let's go get some grub."

At the table Ann looked as if she had swallowed a canary. She could hardly sit still and could talk only about the party the next evening. In between eating and talking she looked at Jack with those bright eyes of hers.

Mrs. Rollin spent dinner beaming at the two of them. Mr. Rollin ate with a grin on his face, and Jack could not figure out how he did it without spitting food all over the place. Every time Chin came in he put more food in front of Jack saying, "Eat . . . eat."

Jack still felt very tired and was so full he did not think he would ever be able to eat again. He felt funny when Ann gave him that special look of hers. He felt he would rather have her call him a Tenderfoot Dude than to look at him that way. Not being able to keep his eyes open anymore, he excused himself and went to bed. For awhile he stared at the ceiling. He saw Ann with her pretty smile and bright eyes; he felt the cowhands slapping him on his back and telling him he was a hero. What was a hero anyway? Well, whatever it was he wasn't it, he decided as he drifted off to sleep.

CHAPTER TWENTY-ONE: The Barn Dance

All the next day people scurried around making preparations for the big party. The old barn was decorated and food was being prepared by Chin, Mrs. Rollin and Pete, who had been called up from the back bunkhouse to help. Ann was supervising the decorations. In fact, no one paid much attention to him. He occasionally saw a couple of the hands whispering and looking at him, which made him nervous. After a lunch filled with people talking about the logistics of the event, Jack went for a ride searching for solitude. He felt as if his life had changed greatly in the last few months. He mulled over the fact that he had faced real danger and overcome his fears. He had learned to be a cowboy —well, almost. He also thought about the feelings he had for Ann. Normally, he thought girls were just a bother, so why didn't he feel that way about her?

When he returned to the ranch house, he found to his great surprise and joy that Frank had returned home.

"Hey! Frank!" Jack yelled when he saw him. "When did to get here?"

"Just now." Frank had such a big grin on his face he could hardly talk. "Is what I've been hearing true?" He pounded Jack on the back.

"Well," Jack said, trying to keep from coughing. "Some of it. Depends on what you heard."

"Come on in the house. I want to hear everything." They went into Jack's room and sat on the bed. Jack told him about riding fence, rustlers, snakes, scorpions and "the only thing that I didn't see was a wild cat." They laughed.

"That was a danged dangerous thing you did, saving Ann," Rich said.

"But I told you it was Whiley who saved us,' Jack insisted.

"That's not how he tells it. He said you headed to the cave by yourself and he followed you there. He went into the cave, but came out looking for help. You, however, went in looking for Ann, but were caught before finding her. Then you were smart enough to cut the rope with a knife he threw to you and lift Ann out of the cavern, giving Whiley time to get Ann safely away. When he came back he had a tug of war with Jed, you being the rope." Frank laughed. "I wish I could have seen that!"

"I give up," Jack said, throwing up his hands in surrender. "I'm just glad you came back."

"I finished my ROTC training yesterday, so here I am. I knew nothing of all this until I arrived home. I'm sure happy you decided to ride fence for us." Frank took Jack's hand. "I'm proud to know a cowpoke like you."

Jack was too embarrassed and happy to say anything.

"Guess we better get ready for the big party," Frank said, heading for his room.

After taking a shower, Jack went back to his room. On the bed was a fancy cowboy shirt. It was light blue, with dark blue shoulders, and had pearl buttons. A new pair of dress pants, dark blue like the other cowpokes wore, lay next to it. At the foot of his bed was a pair of dress boots. They were dark brown and tooled with cactus, which were dyed green and surrounded by a blue sky. When Jack put everything on they fit to perfection. He looked in the mirror and could not believe what he saw: a young cowboy, taller and older looking now. As he looked closely he saw some dark hair fuzz beginning to grow on his cheeks. He would soon have to learn to shave. After one more glance in the mirror, Jack straightened his shoulders and walked through the patio to the family room.

Mr. and Mrs. Rollin were there, seated on the Western style sofa. They grinned at him.

"You sure make a handsome cowboy," Mrs. Rollin said, handing him a small box, which Jack quickly stowed in his pocket. "Watch out for the girls tonight. They are all going to want to dance with you."

Jack wasn't sure he knew how to dance, at least not Western style. In school they had learned a little about line dancing and square dancing, but he could remember nothing about it.

As he was thinking about dancing, he saw Ann. She was so different he hardly recognized her.

She was wearing a beautiful western dance dress. It was blue and yellow checkered, with white lace trim. She must have had a dozen petticoats underneath because the skirt stuck way out. The dress brought out the beauty of her long red hair tied in a ponytail, which reached to her waist. Her eyes sparkled more than they ever had before. He had not known she was such a beauty. Where had his Ann gone and who was this woman?

As she walked into the room, Ann knew her new dress would make a stir, but she forgot that when she saw Jack. He was handsome. She had seen him as an annoying kid at first, then as a friend. But now—now he was a man—a handsome man. Her heart skipped a beat, and she became afraid. Maybe he would not like her anymore. Other girls would surely be attracted to him. She turned red with embarrassment as she thought, *"I'm thinking of Jack as my man."* Her thoughts were interrupted by Frank coming in. Ann quickly compared Jack to her Uncle Frank. Frank was handsome, but Jack was much more attractive.

"Let's go," Frank said. "We'll take the car, although it's not very far. Can't have all these pretty gals getting mussed."

There must have been more than a hundred people at the party. There was a Western band with guitar, banjo, drums, fiddle and bass, and a man to call the moves in square dancing. He remembered some of what he had been taught about square dancing, and Ann was very helpful in making sure he didn't look like a fool.

"Seems as if she wants to dance all the dances with me," he thought. The food, bar-b-que right off the grill—steaks, brisket, hamburgers, chicken and sausages with all the trimmings—were served in the yard outside. His greatest problem was trying not to spill on his new shirt.

The band stopped playing and filed off the stage for a break. Ann, standing beside him, took his hand. Although at first he wanted to withdraw it, instead he gave her hand a squeeze and discovered he liked holding it.

Mr. Rollin ascended to the band stage and raised his hands for silence.

"Ladies and gentlemen," he said over the microphone, "we are here to celebrate the catching of the rustlers that have been bleeding me dry these past two years. We could not have caught them so soon had it not been for Jack over there." He pointed to where Jack was standing. "Come on up here, Jack. I want everyone to see you."

Jack hesitated, his face turning red. He was too embarrassed to go.

"Go on, Jack," Ann said as she gave his hand a squeeze.

He threaded his way to the stage and as he did so people

started clapping and whistling. Men grabbed his arm or hit him on the back in congratulations and some of the girls looked him over good. He did not want the recognition, but he went anyway.

When he reached the stage, Mr. Rollin put his arm over his shoulders. "Not two months ago this young man was a greenhorn. A tenderfoot dude." There was laughter. Jack blushed. "Now he has learned to ride, rope and even to catch rustlers." More laughter. "Frank, you're out there somewhere, come on up."

Frank parted the crowd and came on stage with a box in his hand.

"It was Frank that found this young cowboy, so it is only fitting that he does the honors."

"Jack," Frank said, looking at him. "I knew you would make a good cowboy when you bluffed me out when I had three of a kind and you only had a pair of deuces."

Laughter broke out and someone yelled, "Gotta watch him when playing poker." There was another roar of approval.

Frank quieted the crowd. "You all know we have a Rollin's tradition when a man becomes qualified to be a real cowpoke. We award him his spurs. That's what we are going to do for Jack right now.

"Jack, you have worked hard, not complained, been thrown a few times, learned how to rope, captured some rustlers and at least one girl's heart. Come on up here, Ann."

Jack saw Ann coming through the crowd smiling. She came up to the stage and stood by Jack, taking hold of his hand again.

"Ann, will you make the presentation?" Frank asked. Ann took the box and opened it. She took out a set of beautiful silver spurs. Not the training spurs he had been using, but real ones. They were shaped in a star, each point having a little ball to keep them from hurting the horse.

"Now that you know how to treat a horse, and all the other things that go along with being a cowboy, I present you with these spurs as a symbol of your competence as a cowboy."

Jack, overwhelmed, took the spurs and before he knew it, Ann placed a kiss on his cheek. Again the crowd roared. They started chanting, "Speech, speech!"

Jack walked up to the microphone. The crowd quieted down, ready to hear him speak. For a while he stood, wondering what the heck he was going to say. He knew he had to say something. They were all waiting.

"Uh . . . I appreciate your support. Especially Mr. Rollin, who let me come for the summer and try to be a cowboy. Thank you, Frank, for asking me here and teaching me how to ride. To Pete and his horse-liniment." There was some hooting and laughter from the crowd. Jack swallowed hard and continued.

"I also want to thank Tork and all the guys who had patience with me. I know I've grown a lot this summer. I will be sorry to leave in a couple of weeks." He looked at Ann. "I'll miss you . . . all. I think I've grown taller—but that might be because I was used in a tug of war. And I also feel stronger," Jack grabbed his backside, "especially here." Again the crowd laughed. "I'll not forget any of you. Now I think we should get back to dancing."

After the music started again, Jack took Ann's hand and led her outside. "I think I need some fresh air," he explained. "Let's go for a walk." Ann nodded her agreement.

They walked down the dirt road, hand in hand.

"It's a beautiful night," Ann said, looking up into the sky. "Look at the stars. I feel I could reach out my hand and pluck them like cherries." Jack was deep in thought but gripped her hand a little harder as an answer. "The moon is so big, see?"

"Don't tell me there's going to be smooching!" Austin interjected.

"Shee," Rachael shushed him. "Go on, Grandpa."

Jack looked at the huge moon rising in the east. "Yes, it's a very nice night."

When they came to a big live oak silhouetted against the rising moon, they stopped.

"Brighteyes," he said turning toward her, "I really appreciate your help in all of this. I, uh, want to give you this little present."

Ann opened the box and looked inside. She did not say

anything for a second, and then a sound escaped her lips.

"Ooooo . . . You got it . . .the necklace . . . how did you ever . . . it's just what I've been wanting all summer. She wiped away a tear from her cheek and was silent for a moment. "I didn't do anything," she said, looking at Jack and trying not to make a fool of herself by crying.

"Sure you did," he laughed as he placed the locket chain around her neck. "You made me angry enough to bear all the pain and work it took to learn to ride and rope."

Ann giggled, the moonlight flashing in her bright eyes. "You mean calling you a Tenderfoot Dude?"

"Yeah." He had to look away from her eyes, which were driving him nuts. "That and all the other mean things you did."

"Then why did you save my life?"

"I guess because I like you very much." He drew closer to her.

"I like you a lot too," she said and kissed him on the lips.

Jack was confused. Now things were going around in his mind that never had been there before. He knew he liked the feeling and the kiss. So he kissed her back.

"Wow," Ann said. "That was nice."

"Yes," Jack said, "it was nicer than nice." They turned and walked back to the dance. This time Jack had his arm around her. Not only had he won his spurs, but he had his first real girlfriend and his first kiss.

CHAPTER TWENTY-TWO: "My Summer Vacation"

The next two weeks went too fast. Although riding fence became kind of boring, it was easier too. He missed being with Ann when he was riding. When he came to the ranch house, he and Ann would spend the day having fun, no matter what chores they had to do. Often Frank joined in their outings and horseplay. They talked late into the night about what they wanted to do with their lives.

It was all too soon time to leave. As the day drew near, both he and Ann grew glum. One day as they were riding, Frank rode up and joined them.

"Why so sad?" he asked them.

Both looked up at him, but said nothing.

"Are you unhappy because the summer is over?"

"Yeah," mumbled Jack.

"Hey kids, it's not over," Frank said. "You can keep in touch during the winter and come back next year."

"I can?" Jack asked.

"Of course. We want our newest spurred cowboy back with us next year. Maybe you can take part in the roundup."

Jack looked at Ann and they both smiled.

"Let's go!" Ann cried as she kicked her horse into a joyful gallop.

Frank smiled as he watched his two friends, with Ann in the lead, ride as fast as they could across the field.

After taking leave of the Rollinses and Ann, it took forever for Frank to drive him home. Jack told Frank that he did not think he was cut out to be a cowboy as a profession.

"It's awfully hard work, and dangerous," he explained. "And yet . . . I can hardly wait for next summer. But not because I can be a cowboy, but . . ."

"Because Ann will be there?" Frank finished his sentence.

"Yes. Do you really want me to come back next year?"

"That's right," Frank said. "Sure, we want you back. As for being a cowpoke," he continued, "you will have a lot more opportunities in other fields. If you can win your spurs at the ranch, you can do anything."

"Thanks, Frank," Jack said with a grin.

"But next summer," Frank said, pointing a finger at him, "You will be a cowboy."

When Jack arrived home he was welcomed by his family. Frank told them of Jack's spurs and the heroic deeds he had done. His father beamed and clapped him on the back.

"I knew you could do it. Honey," he said to Jack's mother, "our son's a hero. Did you hear that?"

"I didn't realize he would be in danger, but I'm glad he came home safely," Jack's mother said, forcing a smile through her tears of happiness.

His sister, Dianne, wasn't listening. She just beamed at Frank and was glad the summer was over so she could date him again. This time Jack understood his sister better. And he missed Ann already. How was he going to last almost a year before seeing her again?

Jack told none of his friends of his adventures. He figured they would think he was lying or telling tall stories. Even he could hardly believe what had happened . . . and his success. To remind himself that the summer had not been a dream, he hung his hard won spurs over his bed.

School started and Jack's first class was English. He looked at the black board and read with disgust, "Write an essay about your summer vacation."

Not again! English teachers do not have much imagination. Every year it was the same thing. Taking out his note book, he printed his name on the right side on the paper and in big block letters wrote the title, My Summer Vacation, on the top line.

He looked at the blank paper, wondering what he should write. Could he tell about learning to ride and roping chickens? Could he say that Ann had called him a Tenderfoot Dude? No way! The kids would surely call him that all year.

How could he explain the beauty and fear he experienced

riding fence—his encounters with snakes, scorpions, and rustlers? What about Ann and her beautiful red hair and green eyes? How could he say anything about her when he, himself, was still confused about that kiss they shared?

"Jack" It was his English teacher. "You had better stop staring into space and write your essay."

"Yes , Ma'am." Looking down at his paper again, he began to write.

MY SUMMER VACATION

I went to a ranch and had a good time.
I learned how to ride a horse and met nice
people. It was fun. Maybe next year I'll do it
again.

The End

"He really would have been in trouble telling that he was called Tenderfoot Dude," Austin laughed.

"That was a wonderful story Grandpa," Rachael said, her eyes sparkling with tears. "I really liked that part when Jack gave her the pendant she wanted."

"You probably liked that smoochie kiss too," Austin teased.

"Are you going to tell us another story tomorrow?" Rachael asked, pleading.

"No. The summer is about over and you have to return home soon." Grandpa smiled and, with a shiver, pulled his sweater on and then continued. "But if you make good grades in school this year, I'll tell you the story of *"Jack and the Back Bay Pirates"* when we gather around the fire pit next summer.

That night Austin dreamed of bad cowboys and rustlers. Rachael dreamed of Ann and Jack holding hands and walking in the moonlight. And Grandpa dreamed of cuddling his grandchildren like he had done when they were babies.

ABOUT THE AUTHOR

Ames K. Swartsfager is a priest in the Episcopal Church and has been retired for many years. He is a grandfather to seven children and great-grandfather to four. He loves telling stories to anyone who will sit still enough to hear them.

He lives with his wife, Judy, in Connecticut.

www.ingramcontent.com/pod-product-compliance
Lightning Source LLC
Chambersburg PA
CBHW030336180626
46810CB00003B/1387

* 9 7 8 0 9 8 2 7 5 8 0 3 8 *